THANKS FOR CARING

G. LUSBY

PublishAmerica
Baltimore

First printing

ISBN: 1-4137-3397-2
PUBLISHED BY PUBLISHAMERICA, LLLP
www.publishamerica.com
Baltimore

Printed in the United States of America

Dedication

To my parents Alice and Leonard, who also suffered through a tour of duty in Vietnam; and of course to Patty, without whom this book would never had materialized. It took many months of work, spanning a year, to pull the happy letters and sad memories out of my mind and onto the written page. Many times it hurt deeply to write about my fallen comrades, but writing it down eventually gave me the feeling of dedication, so this is also my written memorial to them.

TO PEG & JOHN -
TWO GOOD FRIENDS FROM
OUR WORKING PAST.
GOOD LUCK IN THE FUTURE -

10/04

PREFACE

In March of 1965 the very first United States combat troops landed at DaNang Air Base in South Vietnam, catapulting us into the longest full-time war our country would ever know. By September of 1968, our troops in Vietnam would total 537,800 men, the largest number of US forces to be in combat there. On August 12, 1972 the last US combat forces left Vietnam, turning the war over to the Vietnamese people. During that time period, the United States would spend approximately 150 billion dollars supporting the war. Our military arsenal would be reduced by some 4865 helicopters and 3720 aircraft, all lost in battle. Our bombers would release a total to exceed 8 million bombs, while our artillery would expend an average of 10,000 artillery shells a day. In the field, a total of 2.9 million men and women would fight in the war for the United States. Of that number, 57,939 US soldiers lost their lives for their country, 300,000 were wounded, 75,000 were permanently injured for life, and 2,500 were missing in action!

I don't believe any of them really wanted to be there. I don't believe any of them were gung-ho enough to like the Vietnam war or why it was being fought. From the time we got our orders to go to Nam, we hated it. When they shot out bodies full of immunizations and sent us into combat, we hated it. When we killed other people and watched ourselves being killed, we hated it. When we left Vietnam without a victory, we hated it. And when we got home and saw what America thought of us, we hated it.

Those of us who were lucky enough to make it home after 395 days in Nam, came home to hatred and bitterness. We were veterans and proud of it, but there was no one to listen. Our country was ashamed of the role it played in the Vietnam war, a war that America chose to fight in, but Americans wanted no part of. We didn't want any part of it either. On July 8, 1959, Major Dale Buis, the first American killed in action in South Vietnam didn't want any part of it. On January 27, 1973, Lt. Colonel William B. Nolde, the last American killed in combat didn't want any part of it. None of us did. But we went, we fought, and over 57,000 of us died. From the moment that Major Dale Buis fell to the ground giving his life for his country, we were committed to make it worth his life. We fought our hearts out for our country and America spit on us. They called it a rock-and-roll war, fought by teenagers who were alcoholics, dope addicts, and murders. Well, they were right!

We were different than other veterans. We were teenagers told to fight a war in a country we never heard of, for a cause no one could explain to us. We were rock-and-rollers from the baby-boom era who wouldn't think twice about putting our lives on the line for our country, but this wasn't our country or our war. Our music was our lifestyle and it's what we related to best, but they took away our radios and handed us rifles, so we fought our battles with the music as our spirit. Given the tensions and stress of war, we celebrated daily with a reward of alcohol. We used its medicinal power to congratulate ourselves for making it through another day, to soothe the worry of what will happen tomorrow, and forget the pain of killing while being killed. Some guys coped in other ways, one of which was marijuana, but they too had their own inner battles to deal with. They too were surrounded by a hostile environment closing in daily, torturing you with barbaric tactics and leaving your comrades lifeless. We were each plucked out of our homeland, away from our families, and asked to fight, yet criticized for the way we handled stress or had some fun. Half of the American students are smoking grass with no stress at all in their daily lives, why are we pointed at and not them? Is it really us, or is it the war we're participating in that irritates the American people.

And murderers? How many times do we make a judgement without really knowing the facts. We won't deny we did some innocent killing, but we also won't deny we were tired of putting the bodies of our comrades in bags to ship home. How many times could we watch innocent women and children give us gifts that would blow up in our faces; how many times could we defend a village and its people only to find them harboring caches of weapons and supplies for the enemy; how many times could we watch a friendly villager by day become an enemy infiltrator by night. It doesn't take too long before you become bitter and lose your compassion. We saved the lives of many, many innocent women and children in village after village, and these occurrences far outnumber the incidents of innocent killings. There were never killings without a purpose. Are we to believe that throughout our two world wars that no innocent citizens were killed for any reason. Is it really that these few incidents happened, or is it the persistent hatred by the American people of this war and therefore a hatred of everything associated with it.

We were rockin'-and-rollin' teenagers who sang, drank, smoked, and killed, but we were also teenagers who matured overnight as we were killed, maimed, and tortured for nothing. Killed to help a people and culture that could really care less whether we were there or not. They had been at war for twenty years so we were just more troops to inhabit their land and destroy their environment.

We really didn't ask much in return—a reason to fight, a little support and encouragement, and a lot of mail. Mail was our connection to home, a home we needed to hear from. Our letters kept us aware of our situation on the homefront, a situation that was filled with demonstrations and peace marches. A home that was filled with hatred. We needed some encouraging words to help us keep our sanity and not give up, the way it seemed most Americans had given up on us and our cause. It was written all over their faces when we returned. We didn't return as "war veterans," we returned as the Vietnam kids who killed innocent people, smoked pot, drank booze, and went over to take part in a war that nobody wanted to be in. The heroes were the guys who fled to Canada and dodged the draft, the heroes were the peace marchers and the students who talked against the war. We were the outcasts!

There were no parades for Vietnam vets. There were no welcome home banners and celebrations except for the families who suffered with us. When people talk of wars we fought throughout history, Vietnam is called the "ugly" war, not because the brutality of the war was deep and endless, but because it was the war no one wanted. The war America fought in and chose to forget.

Ten years after the United States pulled its troops out of South Vietnam, the United States government, with the forceful effort of Vietnam Veterans and their families, decided to recognize the war heroes of Vietnam. On November 13, 1982, the United States dedicated the Vietnam Veterans Memorial in Washington, D.C. to finally pay its respects to those 58,000 men and women who sacrificed their lives for their country in that ugly war. Twelve years after we left Vietnam, on November 11, 1984, the United States erected a monument dedicated to those Americans who fought in our country's longest war; a statue of three US soldiers to overlook the Vietnam Memorial Wall and remind us of the countless individuals who risked their lives for that ugly cause. Also in the same year, 1984, a body was placed in the Arlington National Cemetery. An unknown soldier from the Vietnam war took his final resting place at the Tomb of the Unknown Soldiers of World Wars I and II, and the Korean War. Thirteen years after we all came home, the people of the United States finally remembered us. In May of 1985, a national Vietnam Veterans parade was held in New York City honoring the veterans who fought in the Vietnam war. The parade and welcome home they never received finally took place, over a decade later.

I'm sorry, America...you're too late, the wounds are too deep. Yes, we want to pay our respects to our 58,000 comrades who died at our side for their country. And yes, we want to recognize our 375,000 comrades who brought their suffering back with them and in many cases are paying the highest price a war can inflict, they need our help and our understanding as they tackle their pain daily. And yes, we want you to find our 2,500 missing comrades who are still over there and may well be paying the biggest price of all, if they are still alive. But basically, you're too damn late! We needed your support then, much more than we need your support now. We needed the support you gave to our World War I, World War II, and Korean war vets, who fought their hearts out not just for 395 days, but for years in battle without coming home. America was behind them and they knew it, we knew the opposite.

Vietnam was ugly. But it was the war that was ugly, not the men who fought in it. Did we deserve to eat the mud and dirt of Vietnam for over a year of our lives fighting a battle our country put us in, then come home and be ignored, ridiculed, and forgotten. Ask a Vietnam vet, he'll tell you Nam was ugly, but America was uglier.

This book is dedicated to the Patty Chapman's of the world. The people who took the time to care, when they really didn't have to. She wasn't involved in the war. The families of the American soldiers fighting overseas were involved in the war, they had a stake in it. But not the Patty Chapman's. She wrote to me because she cared about me. She cared about the guys around me and what we were doing. Sure, maybe she hated the Vietnam war too, who wouldn't hate a war, but that didn't stop her from caring about the guys who were from her country, fighting a war they didn't want to be in either. Was she really so different than anyone else, who knows, but she took the time to care.

I have no doubt in my mind that I survived the Vietnam war and came home to my family because of Patty Chapman. Her letters took me through times that I never dreamed I could survive. The pain of a war and the suffering, both mentally and physically, is insurmountable. Ask any vet from any war. Times that I suffered the most from losing my buddies, my life was at an all time low. It takes an overwhelming force to pick you up and tell you that you must go on, you must continue, it will be over soon. That force was a Patty Chapman letter. Her dedication, to not only write me continually for a year, but to do it almost daily, is astounding. She is a remarkable woman and to her I owe my life. The Vietnam Veterans Memorial was needed, the parades were appreciated, but the Patty Chapman's are to be saluted. This book is my memorial to her. Thanks, Patty. *Thanks For Caring!*

THE BEGINNING

Why is the beach such a beautifully quiet, exciting place for two people to share their enchanting moments together? It seems the emptiness of this vast stretch of desert is overflowing with the romantic qualities necessary for an intimate evening. Two figures can be seen silhouetted against the falling sunset as if they were placed there for the purpose of adding meaning to the word beauty.

The orange-redness of the warm misty sky completely outlining two shadows of nature, which are silently conveying more intimate messages than a book could hope to reveal. Hand in hand, only their silence comes between them as they walk mile upon mile, yet meaning has replaced tiredness.

The atmosphere of the entire environment is a perfection no man could ever hope to create himself. The long, white, empty beach lying helpless as the coldness of tons of ocean water crash down upon it, creating surf which dissipates into the sands' warmness. Sand, cold in the night, as your footprints compress the water out with every step you take. Sand that oozes between your toes by day as you scamper across its scorching hotness; but becomes hard and cold with the downward movement of the sun. The complete silence of this world interrupted only occasionally by the echoing of the waves striking the beach...a sound which only enhances the entire scene more.

Suddenly with this sound, all nature is alive and all the world has meaning. Two figures gazing at each other for the first time, introducing themselves to each other through the silence of their touch. They meet, eyes focused in each other's stare, they join hands and become united as one. Their warmness and breathing communicate their inner feelings as words could not hope to. The pounding surf interrupts the silence but enhances the meaning as suddenly the entire atmosphere is perfect and the two silhouettes become one. The dream of mankind is captured in this one moment as man and woman are one, together.

There are different kinds of love shared by two people, from the basic love of friendship, to the whole-hearted dedicated love between a man and a woman. But I think I have experienced a love with more meaning and sincerity than two people could ever imagine. It is truly rare to love someone for inner beauty with no physical attraction or personal characteristics in any way being influential, but I feel that a beautiful relationship of this kind became my thread of survival while overseas in Vietnam. Fourteen thousand miles away from a girl who would soon become a part of me and would someday bring my beach scene to reality.

It was a hot muggy day in June of 1965 that a decision was made on my part, to endanger my life, enrich my manhood, and be "dictatorized" for the next three years of my young life. I painstakingly enlisted in the United States Marine Corp to "see the world"...which turned out to be North Carolina, California, and South Vietnam.

I had graduated from high school in June of 1964 and decided to bum around for the summer and enjoy some real freedom for a change. What more could a guy ask for...a high school diploma in-hand, a like-new 1959 Pontiac Star Chief to drive, living at home in an upstairs apartment with no bills, plenty of good fun-loving friends, and a steady girl by my side. Wow!

I spent the better part of the summer cruising around the favorite spots of the city, like Ameches, the Hot Shoppes, Champs, and the other fast-food drive-ins of our time. After you had spent the better part of the day shining up your car, you'd pull in to each drive-in and cruise around four or five times to show off your wheels. After a while you would place a food order through a speakerphone and before you knew it, some groovy-lookin' chick with a short, short skirt and a sweater that just wouldn't quit, would bring your order out to you. She'd hook the food tray to the window of your car and when you were finished, you'd usually forget and drive off with the tray still hangin' out the side of your car.

We would spend hours upon hours in these places just checking out the cars and of course, checking out the girls. If things weren't hot there we would just cruise to the next place. Of course gas back in those days was about twenty to twenty-five cents a gallon, so two bucks usually filled up the ol' gas tank and provided enough cruisin' for days.

Towards the end of summer I decided to go back to school, but couldn't quite bring myself to make the full commitment to a four-year college; so junior college it was. Two years sounded so much better than four, especially after just finishing twelve years of school.

Life in college turned out to be much different than the dull humdrum days of high school, where every day was a commitment and you were going because you had to, not because you wanted to. Now you attended for your own reasons, whether they be for self-betterment, college life, or just for the stupid piece of paper that was so important in the working world. But after two semesters I could see that college was not in my immediate plans just yet. I needed something to break the everyday routine in my life. I was going through the motions of college life, but it was for the social benefits, not the educational advantages.

Enter Stan, my best friend at the time, or should I say I thought he was my best friend. He came up with the brilliant idea of enlisting in the Marine Corp in the "buddy" plan, which meant that we would stay together through boot camp and infantry training. Well, needless to say I was vulnerable, and before too long we were signing our names for three years of active duty. But being the fantastic organization that the armed forces is, they gave us the entire summer off and told us to report on September 18 to begin our 'new life.' Need I say that the summer was spent cruisin' on the streets, tanning on the beach, parking in the woods, and drinkin' up a storm!

But September came much too fast and before we knew it we

were whisked away to Parris Island, South Carolina for twelve weeks of boot camp, Marine Corp style. Ouch…what have I done to myself! Stan, I'll kill you for this…buddy!

The Marine Corp Recruit Depot—Parris Island, South Carolina—hell on earth. From the moment our bus pulled through the depot gates until we pulled up to the receiving barracks, Stan and I must have puffed away a pack of cigarettes apiece. We figured it would probably be our last 'freedom' for a while…it would be!

As our bus came to a stop, we got our first glance at our new mother, father, and ruler for the next two months. Standing firm and rigid, tall and proud, with his hands clasped behind him, was the man who would strip us of every bit of human dignity we had accumulated in our young lives. His uniform was sharp, neat, and letter perfect, his Smokey Bear hat positioned exactly on the top of his head.

As he boarded the bus, our smiles and chatter slowly disappeared as we realized the huge mistake we had made.

"Okay, shut-up and listen. You maggots will grab your bags and whatever other belongings you have and move your ass off this bus as fast as you can. When I say go, I better see every swinging dick moving off this bus in a split second. You will move off this bus and line your pitiful bodies up on the yellow footprints out on my Marine Corp pavement. Each one of you had better be standing on a set of yellow footprints and not standing on my Marine Corp pavement, and your mouths better not be moving."

He turned and got off the bus.

"Go!"

It was like a mob scene as we flew out the bus doors onto the sidewalk. I can remember standing directly behind my "buddy" Stan and whispering, "What the hell did you get me into?"

From that moment on, we were demoralized to the level of pond scum and slowly began our uphill journey towards a Marine Corp spit and polished man. The Marine Corp philosophy is to completely wash your mind of everything and start you off as dirt. Every moment of every day you are convinced by your superiors that you are the scum of the earth and are labeled with the name "maggot." They reduce you to chores and duties that take the mentality of a rock and what rewards you get you earn sparingly. As time goes by, you are restructured their way in both mind and body. Each day is a new experience, from the morning awakening as a metal trash can is thrown down the aisle of your barracks to wake you up, to the daily chore of cleaning the barracks with a toothbrush. They shaved our heads, stripped our dignity, drained our minds, forced us back to our childhood, and began building our minds and bodies to fit the Marine Corp mold. Upon leaving boot camp you are by far mentally prepared for Marine Corp life and physically prepared for manhood. When the day of final graduation arrives, it marks a day no Marine will ever forget as long as they live. You have made it through twelve weeks of hell, humiliation, torture, and mental anguish, and have built a new mind, body, and manliness. You are now a Marine. You stand tall, you stand proud of what you have accomplished, and a shiver comes over your body as the Marine Corp Hymn is played, because now it is your hymn.

My next stop was four weeks of advanced infantry training at beautiful Camp Lejeune, North Carolina, the armpit of the world. This phase of our training was to familiarize us with the wonderful world of combat, weapons, and survival in the field. This part was certainly not as bad as boot camp because now we were at least treated like human beings, and besides, in a matter of weeks we would be going home. Aaaahhhh, thirty days leave!

My orders took me back to Camp Lejeune for a while where I pulled some administrative duty for a couple of months, but finally my orders came through and I was shipped out for twenty weeks of radio-telegraph school at the Marine Corp Recruit Depot...are you ready for this...in sunny, warm San Diego, California. Home of the famous California girls!

Now, California was fun! I came out to San Diego a Private First Class and twenty weeks later left a Lance Corporal, which ain't half bad for someone who was havin' a pretty good time in the Sunshine State. I bought myself a car, a 1957 Chevy, of course, and spent five glorious months introducing myself to the wonderful world of west coast women.

The one thing that I did get out of radio-telegraph school, besides a thorough understanding of a radio and an instantaneous recognition of Morse Code, was a nickname; instead of being Gary to everyone, I picked up the name 'G.' For some reason there was this black guy, Lorenzo, who called a lot of guys by the first letter of their name…with me it just stuck.

After finishing school and going back home on leave for a while, I received my orders to Vietnam. I was to report to Camp Pendleton, California for four weeks of advance combat training, then we were to fly out on November 18 for Okinawa, and on to DaNang air field in South Vietnam.

We received some fantastic training at Camp Pendleton, all to prepare us for live combat situations. We fired every weapon imaginable, tossed every kind of grenade made, got fired at with every size bullet created, ate everything from powdered milk to cold dry beans, went days without a shower, and got dropped off in the middle of a desert/jungle with a compass and told to find our way home. Well, there was no way I thought I could walk from California to Maryland, so I just worked my way back to base camp.

It was called survival training and that's exactly what it was. We were taught how to live off the land and how to make the most of any situation. To do that, we were required to walk twenty-five miles with full backpack gear without stopping; told to tread water in full gear for two hours, which they called drown-proofing; and repeatedly reminded of the military code of conduct which stated that we were responsible to know only our name, rank, and serial number if captured by enemy forces. Not once did they tell us to love thy neighbor!

Needless to say, we were mentally prepared and scared shitless!

For the first time in my entire life I boarded a plane that took off on time…great, of all times to get it right! We flew from Edwards Air Force Base to Honolulu, Hawaii, where we were allowed to wander the airport for thirty minutes while the plane refueled. It was like the calm before the storm...beautiful, serene, pleasant Hawaii here, with hustling, ugly, military-structured Okinawa there. After a fourteen hour flight we arrived there to be staged for transportation into Vietnam, our home for the next thirteen months.

On November 21, 1966, I landed at DaNang air field in South Vietnam. DaNang was a large American airbase which was situated on the eastern coast of South Vietnam bordered by the South China Sea to its east, and mountains to its south and north. Strategically it was in the I Corps region, which was the northernmost military region in South Vietnam, midway between the demilitarized zone (DMZ) and the borderline of the II Corps region just to the south of Chu Lai and My Lai. The main highway in Nam, Route 1, ran directly through DaNang making it a hustling complex full of military and civilian activity. The airstrip consisted of two long concrete runways stretching north and south across the Tien Sha peninsula and was bordered by a sprawling jumble of prefabricated buildings, sandbagged barracks, and large metal storage facilities. The entire area was a frenzy of pandemonium with a flurry of activity from planes, helicopters, motorized vehicles, bicycles, and every other imaginable form of transportation.

As we left our plane and walked single-file down the ramp, the sweltering heat of Southeast Asia hit us smack in the face. The tropical heat and stenchy smell that filled the air grabbed you by the throat and welcomed you to South Vietnam. Dust was rising from the road with the movement of every object as I glanced from right to left, checking out everything in sight. The entire area was bustling with activity as each one of us slowly made our way into the land that was now our new home for the next year. A drab olive green bus pulled up beside our bewildered column and we were instructed to get aboard for our short journey to the "processing center," located deeper in the compound. We headed out and before long pulled beside a group of metal huts and proceeded to file out with our seabags in hand.

As the bus pulled away we stood like a group of newborn pups left alone for the first time without their mother. Looking around we slowly headed towards a building marked processing center, slowly marching single file as we had done routinely for the past year or so. As we passed, other Marines laughed at us as we marched by fresh and clean, starched and pressed, neat and trim, but lost and bewildered. They were all the opposite. Their war-torn faces were dirty and sweaty as they passed, a walking arsenal of bullets, grenades, and weapons strapped around their necks and waists. The once clean, pressed military fatigues they wore were now soaked and stained by the "Nam experience." Their style and mannerisms that were once strictly military were now controlled by the salt of the war. They were still all boys—boys eighteen, nineteen, twenty years old, with traces of war scarred on their faces. Boys forced to become men by facing death and learning to accept it. We would become that way soon…I could sense what we were in for.

"Hey cherries, hope you're ready to find out what hell is like, cause that's exactly where you are!" shouted a raunchy looking Marine who looked like he hadn't shaved, showered, or changed clothes since he'd been over there.

"Yea, just what we been waitin' for, more FNG's to add to the scenery over here," laughed his buddy. I didn't know what he meant by FNG but it wouldn't take long for me to find out that it stood for Frigin' New Guy, my new designation. As always in life, every new chapter that you open puts you in as low guy on the totem pole, and here I was again. Why is life like that? Every new school you go to you're the new kid on the block; every new job you start you're always the rookie; you work your way to the top, move ahead, and you're put right back on the bottom again. Great, I had gone from maggot, to a slug, to a green private, to a new radio school graduate, to a fresh combat-ready piece of slime, and now a cherry frigin' new guy. I couldn't wait to see what I'd become next!

The whole area was a hot, dusty, unfriendly place, with everyone too occupied with what they were doing to pay any attention to us. I could hear the sounds of explosions in the distance that re-enforced the fact that were definitely in a war zone, and the group of us couldn't help but continually look over our shoulders in the direction of the noise. Everyone around us paid no attention to the explosions whatsoever, as if they didn't even hear what was happening. We were scared, they were conditioned!

I stayed at the airstrip that night with the guys I flew in with and in the morning we were given our orders to our assigned unit. I was to report to the 4th Battalion, 12th Marines, Headquarters Battery Artillery Unit, positioned in Dong Ha, just three miles south of the DMZ. Their area of operations (AO), known as "Leatherneck Square," was supposedly a hot spot which supported Dong Ha, Quang Tri, Con Thien, Cam Lo, and the DMZ – all at once. Oh boy!

My first three days in Vietnam were different to say the least. I was issued all the normal Vietnam gear including lightweight tropical fatigues with nice big pockets to carry lots of ammo and grenades to throw at the bad guys; a big heavy helmet all nice and camouflaged to hide my head so no one will know I'm here; two pair of canvas and leather jungle boots with steel toes and metal soles so the booby-trapped punji sticks won't go through my feet; one rain poncho and liner to battle the elements of the monsoon rains; one flak-jacket, a battle vest made of heavy filled fiberglas to keep all the shrapnel and other goodies from getting to my body; an M-16 rifle, which I had just vaguely seen at Camp Pendleton (I had trained on an M-14 with a nice wood stock and some weight to it, this was like a Mattel toy); a Marine Corp green cartridge belt to hold my precious clips of ammo for my toy rifle; the usual supply issue of a metal plate, fork, spoon, knife, cup, and canteen; and my very own green canvas fold-up cot to park my tired body when I wasn't fighting for life, liberty, and the pursuit of happiness.

The camp itself was laid out pretty nice for being in a combat zone, with large green canvas tents situated throughout the main campsite, strategically surrounded by sandbagged bunkers and fortified positions for each of the artillery gun emplacements. The unit had been in Dong Ha for about nine months, so it was strongly implanted into the hillside and ready for whatever action was thrown at it.

Dong Ha itself was also strategically placed on Route 1 at the junction to Route 9 which led to Khe Sanh, about nine miles to the west. Quang Tri, also on Route 1, was about three miles to our south, and Con Thien, the closest installation to the DMZ was two miles to our northwest. The DMZ itself laid three miles north and ran east and west following the Ben Hai river. It was a barren, uncivilized area about eight hundred meters wide and twelve miles long, full of pot holes, bomb craters, and purposely providing a buffer zone between North and South Vietnam at the 17th parallel.

It was during this introductory period at Dong Ha that I probably did more for my body than any other time in my life, except for the nights Carol and I spent at the drive-in movies! The reason for the body building lesson was a simple item known as a sandbag. Dong Ha had to be the sandbag capital of the world; which was fine for us because being three miles from the DMZ we needed all the protection we could get, fun or no fun. The Marine Corp was really changing me though; I entered boot camp as a 126 pound semi-weakling, and left 12 weeks later as a 152 pound semi-average guy. Now, with this sandbagging bonanza I know I at least doubled my arm size and total strength. So who said Vietnam was a waste of time!

It was here in Dong Ha that I was introduced to some of the greatest guys I have ever known in my life. It was rough at first because being the new guy on the hill you really had to prove yourself and earn your trust and dependability. At first you're strictly known as the replacement for Bill the short-timer, the guy who is next to go home. They've all got "so-many days and a wake-up," you've got a year and a wake-up. But after you do prove yourself and get to know the guys you'll be living with for the next thirteen months, you really learn to appreciate what the term friendship means.

I met a lot of guys during my tour of Nam, but none that bring back the memories and camaraderie as Diff and Joe. Diff was a corporal and had been in Nam for three months when I got there. We hit it off pretty fast because he was from Maryland also, down around Glen Burnie. His real name was Ted Differman, but everyone called him Diff for short. The other guy was Joseph Scalia from the Queens in

New York. He was a lance corporal like me and arrived in Nam about two weeks before I did. Throughout my entire tour of duty overseas no one would have more of an impact on my life than these two guys. Or so I thought!

Dong Ha was really a nothing place, just a name on a map, that happened to be three miles south of the DMZ. It wasn't really a city, or at least I never saw one. We were just on a hill and completely surrounded by dense jungle and even more dense jungle. It didn't take long to adjust to the life of an artillery unit, once you got used to the noise that is. I have never in my life seen guns so big and so loud. Most of our guns were 150mm howitzers with a pretty good range, but our big gals were the 105mm howitzers that could knock the top off a mountain four miles away. Just the shells of these things weighed about 45 pounds each. They did provide quite a safe feeling though; nice to know they were ours and they're pointed out, not in!

Our unit was directed by a First Lieutenant Ron Barton, who was a pretty okay guy. Things are so much different overseas than at stateside. You don't constantly have the petty-ass nit-pickin' shit to put up with overseas, everything isn't just "by the book" the way it is in the states; everyone is a human being and you do things because you want to, not because you have to. Officers are the same way—you don't have to spend half your day saluting every time somebody with some rank walks by. If you do salute, you do it because you really respect the guy, not because you have to. That's the way Lieutenant Barton was, a straight kind of guy who would treat you right if you treated him right. I became pretty close with the lieutenant because I was his radio operator whenever we went out on patrol or convoy. He was a young guy, about twenty-four, well built but stocky, and lived in Connecticut back in the states.

Under Lieutenant Barton was Staff Sergeant Danson and under him was Sergeant Whitt. Danson was kind of the leader of the outfit, he was on his second tour of duty in Nam and knew just about everything you needed to know to survive. He was an older guy, about thirty-six or seven, with an auburn mustache and on the skinny side, but strong as can be. He had one dominate characteristic and that was his love of good US of A alcohol. Just about all of us over there smoked and drank quite a bit, but no one could even think of keeping up with Danson when he started drinking. Have no fear, when the time came for him to perform as a soldier in combat, you never had to worry whether he could function or not because he was the most dependable leader there was. But boy could he have a good time when the coast was clear!

Sergeant Whitt was a good sergeant, but more of an average Joe than a leader. He certainly had all of our respect and could get us to do anything that needed to be done, but he was a lot closer to us guys than he was to Danson and Barton. The kind of sergeant you wanted around whenever something was bothering you or you were in trouble.

Most of the other guys were ordinary type guys; Lenny, Mike, John, Bill, Tony, Mo, and the rest, all good guys just wanting to go home. Lenny was really the senior ranking corporal of the group with about two months left before he would go home. Then came Mike, who never let anyone forget how much time he had in Nam and when he'd be going home. The rest of the guys were a mix of corporals, lance corporals, and PFC's. But even after being over there a couple of days I could tell that Diff was really the leader of the group and the guy most everyone respected and looked up to, even though he had less time in country than Lenny or Mike.

Being close to the DMZ we would get hit quite a bit by the bad guys. In the three weeks I was with the unit in Dong Ha, we got hit about once every other night, but it was really a mediocre attempt to mortar us by some small Viet Cong patrol. It was pretty rare that a small unit with mortars would attempt to hit an artillery unit of the size we were. Mortar flashes were really easy to spot and once located they could easily be abolished with a few well placed rounds. It was a good experience for me, though; I hadn't seen much combat to that point, so a very passive, non-destructive attack was the kind I'd vote for.

Well, just as I was getting use to the surroundings of beautiful Dong Ha, our unit got the word to pack up and move down south to a town known as Phu Bai, just south of the Imperial City of Hue. I was kind of glad to hear we were moving further south, the DMZ was far too close to North Vietnam for me, the further away from the enemy, the better…little did I know this was just the beginning.

CHRISTMAS IN NAM

As our convoy of vehicles moved slowly down Highway 1, we could see the city of Hue off in the distance. Our otherwise unnoticed caravan was now beginning to draw the attention of many civilians, who were hastily carrying their trade into Hue for another endless day of selling and bartering.

One of our biggest responsibilities at Phu Bai would be to not only cut off the supply routes from the north to the south, but to give protection and support to the city of Hue and its many civilians and militia troops. This city was very sacred to the Vietnamese because it was once the Imperial Capital of the old unified Vietnam. With a population exceeding 140,000, it was easily the third largest city in South Vietnam, and had always been a city of culture and military importance due mainly to its accessibility to the South China Sea. Cutting in from the sea flowed the Perfume River, a source of both civilian trade boats and military supply traffic. On its northern bank was the Citadel, the old Imperial Palace, surrounded by huge concrete walls built during the 1800s by both Vietnamese and French forces.

As we drove down its tree-lined streets, we were greeted by groups of school children hastily running an olympic pace to keep up with us. Shy, mysterious, yet beautiful college girls, with long silky black flowing hair, hiding their faces behind a pointed hat as we drove by. And young ambitious boys with their arms extended and hands grasping for candy, goodies, cigarettes, or whatever we would toss their way.

As we approached the southern end of the city, we slowly made our way out of the bustling town that seemed to be so out of place in this barren country, and into the poorer peasant side of town, much more normal to this culture and land. The streets suddenly became overflowing with a sea of vendors and tradesman, peddling their articles to everyone passing by. People selling goods of all kinds, from shoes, sandals, shirts, pants, and hats, to edibles such as fruits, vegetables, chickens, snakes, turtles, fish, shrimp, and rats. Yes, rats! Vietnam has so many damn rats living in the acres of rice paddies, that they now trap them and sell the huge gray rodents as delicacies. Just what I want, a heaping plate of chopped up simmered rat. No thanks! The wicker cages full of live chickens and ducks were much more my speed, at least I could relate to eating them.

As our convoy made its way out of the last small village, we crossed yet another in an endless stream of bridges. This last bridge, a strong bold structure, so out of place in this poor frail barren country, seemed to be symbolic with its presence. It seemed too out of place to be put there just to link two sides of a river; too out of place to support the scurry of foot traffic and the occasional vehicle that drove across. I sensed the small safe little village on one side and the hostile vastness of an unchartered open wilderness on the other, were unwillingly tied together by this huge structure. So much an intrusion by man, placed in the tranquility of nature.

By far the biggest difference between Dong Ha and Phu Bai is the overall security of the area. Phu Bai had been secured by our troops for some time now and entering the compound was like walking into the streets of civilization after being brought up in a primitive tribe in the deep dark jungles of Africa.

Green tents were now replaced by rows and rows of screened wooden hoochies; small hand-dug fox holes had now grown to huge sand-bagged bunkers that wound through the area like a maze of connecting tunnels; huge howitzer guns that once were camouflaged and protected by the green branches of mother nature now would be set into massively built bunkers cut into the ground and encircled by sand-bagged walls four to six layers thick. The entire compound was like a miniature city with large mess halls, fire direction control centers to monitor and control all artillery action and enemy movement, and even a beer-hooch for evening entertainment like some hefty drinking. It was obvious we were taking over an area that had been secured quite some time ago and had been built up through the months by the ever popular Seabee's, the Navy construction engineers.

Each hooch, built to hold about twelve guys, had a tin roof and plywood floor and stood about twenty-four inches off the ground for water and pest control. The sides were plywood up from the floor about three feet, then screen up to the ceiling. At the top of each screen were rolls of black plastic which could be unrolled in the evening hours to conceal the light from within. With the plastic rolled up during the day the screen provided not only the comfort of what breezes there were, but great protection from the bugs and mosquitoes which are ever-present in this hot tropical weather zone. At each end of the hooch were screen doors instead of tent flaps that actually had real true-to-life hinges and closed with a bang after you went through them. Not to mention real working electricity with honest to goodness G.E. light bulbs. Aaaahhhh the life of the rich and famous!

It took us about twelve hours to unload and unpack the trucks and convert this pleasantly strange barren environment into our new home. All the major functions of our unit were set up first, including the command post, artillery sectors, medic, supply tents, and most importantly the mess hall. As things quickly came together, we concentrated on getting our individual hooches divided and set up and as the sun was going down we were settling in to make ourselves as much at home as we could.

Diff, Joe, and I elected to bunk together and chose an appropriate hooch halfway between the mess hall and the beer hall. Hey, we all have our priorities! Since the size of our unit was no where near as large as the unit we replaced, we decided to bunk up into eight-man hooches and give each other lots of room to "live in." We each had a typical Marine Corp issue fold up cot, a two-by-four wooden or metal foot locker, and that's it. By dividing the hooch up into eighths we had an immense amount of area and it seemed almost uncanny that we could really have a place like this in a place like this.

After just three weeks in Dong Ha, where I felt as secure as a chicken in a den of hungry wolves, I now had a small faint feeling of security instead of the uneasy nauseating feeling of being surrounded by groups of sneaky little slant-eye rats dressed in black pajamas carrying Russian-made weapons.

Little did I know that there in Phu Bai, South Vietnam, I would fall in love with a dream. When I arrived in this god-forsaken country, I couldn't imagine in my wildest dreams that I could fall in love with anything over here except maybe some paperwork returning me back home to The World (the GI term for the United States). But I would. I would fall in love with the dream of knowing a girl I had never met, never seen, never talked to, and yet a love would blossom that would be beyond any expectations I could have imagined.

It was December 1966 and the talk of the camp was Christmas, Christmas, Christmas! How could anyone get in the spirit of the holidays with the temperature 104 degrees in the shade, needless to say we were fourteen thousand miles from anyone who even remotely resembled family? But here it was the twelfth month of the year and as tradition would have it, Christmas no matter where you were.

Where the hell was Bob Hope…I'm overseas, so where's he at? I mean, how many years upon years did I spend parked in front of a television set at Christmas time forced to watch Bob Hope and his parade of sex machines put on a show for the troops? Now I'm not saying he shouldn't be commended for his many years of effort because he certainly should, but now it's my turn, so where's he at?

Well, we really knew we wouldn't get to see a big show like his because they wouldn't let him come any further north than DaNang—too much action. But we did hear that another show was coming to our area which was being sponsored by a California disc jockey. I told you I loved the Sunshine State! It would be a small traveling show with three or four performers; but who were we to care how big the show was…it was "live" entertainment from the good ole' US of A. and had real live music and real true to life girls. Girls with big round eyes and long blonde hair; girls without pointed hats on their head; girls without long black silk pajamas on; and girls with the shape of a real female, not the shape of a zipper. Wow! A dream come true!

It was a Sunday when the show finally was to take place and we all crowded into an area where we had built a mock stage and cleared a large area for plenty of guys to stand. The disc jockey who was known as "The Surf Man," ran the show and turned out to be a pretty good stand-up comedian. Of course, after being in Nam for any length of time, laughter and humor were not a common occurrence so just about anything was funny. There was one other comedian who cracked everyone up with his slap-stick routines and sick jokes knocking the military brass, which everyone but the brass thought was funny.

Following the comedians were a couple of country singers, followed by a folk singing duo, all of which we enjoyed, especially the girl singer who had blonde hair, huge round blue eyes, and wore a baby blue short cut string outfit that left exactly nothing to the imagination. I could not tell you one single song she sang. I can't even tell you her name, I don't know. She could have just walked on the stage and stood there smiling, that's all we needed and she had us in the palm of her hand. One girl with about two hundred guys in love with her. Almost heaven!

The star of the show was the famous actress Tippy Hedren. She was really a knockout and looked exactly like she did on the screen…blonde, thin, and beautiful. She kind of did nothing, just played straight man for the disc jockey the way the starlets always did with Bob Hope. She just kind of batted her eyes, rolled her hips, and teased us to death. My only complaint was that she wore long slacks which I'm sure covered up some real beautiful legs. Being the leg man that I am, I really hated those slacks!

The show was over in about an hour and a half and they apologized for the shortness but they had a lot of stops to make and a lot of servicemen to entertain in a short amount of time. Besides, they didn't want to stay in one place too long for fear they would become the target of the day.

We of course understood that and thoroughly voiced our appreciation for what seemed like twenty minutes of continuous applause, whistling, clapping, howling, and groaning. A real nice touch at the end was their coming down into the audience afterwards for autographs, pictures, and just plain old American chatter. As appreciative as we were for them coming over here to entertain us, they couldn't stop thanking us for what we were giving up for them. They really made us feel like we were appreciated by the total American public who backed us and knew what we were over there fighting for...freedom of the people.

At the end each of us were given a small net bag from the Red Cross as a Christmas gift from back home. The bags contained mostly toilet articles, writing supplies, American mementos, and each one had the name and address of the stateside girl who contributed in putting together these dandy little packets. Mine was from a girl in Pensacola, Florida named Patty Chapman who worked for the Southern Bell Telephone Company, which apparently sponsored this entire batch of presents. Each of the girls contributed their own time on behalf of the company to package the articles and get them ready for "our boys overseas." Mine had a nice little note in it from Patty.

> *I hope everything is going as fine with you as it possibly can and we are out of this terrible war as soon as possible. You guys deserve to be home with your families and loved ones during this holiday season and I hope its not too long before that hope comes true. I hope this small Christmas package will in some way help you through these trying times and bring you just a little bit of holiday spirit. We all support you in your daily activities and hope you all make it home safely. I am enclosing my home address*

and would love to hear from you and learn a little bit about the guy who got my note. Thanks and hurry home, Patty.

It was really a fantastic gesture by everyone involved with Southern Bell Telephone Company to take the time to package these gifts and remember us during the holiday season. A season when everyone should be giving thanks for their blessings, but all we could do was curse the system and kill the enemy. I guess our blessing was that we were alive and should be thankful for that, but it's tough to get in the spirit while continuously looking over your shoulder wondering if the person approaching is friend or foe.

Christmas passed and before we knew it we were in the new year 1967. We spent New Year's Eve drinking up most of the American whiskeys that had been sent to the guys through the mail. As time progressed overseas, you learned the best techniques for having things sent to you through the mail. The best way to have whiskey sent was to hollow out a loaf of bread and put the bottle inside the loaf, this would protect the bottle, hopefully. I guess out of about four bottles that I had sent to me only one was shattered when I opened it; it wasn't too much of a mess because the bread had absorbed most of the whiskey…sure was damn good bread though!

The highlight of our New Year's night was another of our wild and crazy card games. We usually played cards just about every pay day, it was our escape from the normal military day. Acey-deucy was the most popular game, where two cards were turned up to you and you made a bet that the next card would be between the two; if it didn't, you had to match the pot. It usually turned up some pretty good pots and the avid gamblers in our unit really looked forward to these nights.

Most of the guys wouldn't keep too much spending cash with them; most of their checks were sent home with enough money kept out for laundry, cigarettes, toilet articles, haircuts, and drinking. With cigarettes costing us a quarter a pack, laundry about a buck a week, and a haircut a dollar a month, it didn't take much money to survive in Nam. So, most of the money was spent either on booze or entertainment, like card playing.

The only thing that you needed to consider was money for R&R (Rest & Relaxation) if you planned on taking it when it was your turn. You were entitled to R&R after you had been in combat about six to eight months but it was usually hard to get unless guys turned it down. The service would pay for your flight and hotel bill, but all the extra curricular activities and souvenirs were at your own expense. The choices available for R&R were Bangkok, Hong Kong, Taipei, Australia, or Hawaii. Most of the married guys would go to Hawaii and meet their families for seven days, but the majority of single guys would go to the Orient figuring it would probably be their only chance to see the Far East, and mingle with the cute little Oriental girls.

Time seemed to pass ever so slowly and life in Phu Bai became pretty routine for each one of us. As radio operator for Lieutenant Barton, our daily routine was to board a Huey chopper every morning and comb the area for sightings of enemy movement and suspected infiltration routes that our artillery could hit that night during our H&I (Harassment and Interdiction) sessions. The chopper would take us over the sites we had hit the night before to inspect the damage if any, and using the reports from our patrols in the area, we would plot coordinates to be hit by our artillery in the wee hours of the morning. Once I became accustomed to flying in the Huey, and the fear of being shot down over the jungle left me, this became my favorite part of the military day. The Huey is definitely an amazing machine, one that you gain an immense amount of respect for and learn quickly to depend on in crucial situations. As I mentioned Phu Bai was a fairly secure area so flying in the chopper certainly wasn't like being down south in the Delta where every trip in the air was filled with gunfire and exploding shells. No thanks, I'll take Phu Bai!

As the months went by, our camp became a home away from home. The hooches we lived in were fixed up great and everyone's area had that certain homespun touch that spelled out each guys feelings. Each area was so riddled with remembrances and mementos from our real homes that it almost seemed like walking into a memorabilia gallery depicting the different life styles of each guy and his family. Seven of the eight cots had State flags hung over them; two Maryland, one New York, two Florida, one Texas, and one Maine…the eighth cot was Ron's and he was still waiting for his flag from Arkansas. It was real easy to get a state flag, just drop a note to your state congressman, tell him you're in Nam and you want a flag, that's it.

The rest of each area was personalized by each guy to satisfy his memories. Most of us had shelves built over our foot lockers with everything on them from pictures of the family back home to newspapers or books sent from the states, and just about everyone had that one special picture of either their wife or sweetheart. My folks had sent me a small tape recorder and I had that on my shelf along with numerous tapes containing the latest songs from back home. It was great hearing the latest songs, but it was the old songs that drove us crazy. Once an old song started playing you could look around the hooch and see the minds wandering to where they were when they heard that song last. Memories were really tough to deal with overseas, but it was really all you had to keep you going, the memories of the people back home and what was waiting for you when you got back.

Each guy, once in Nam for a while, had written home with lists of things that he needed to ease his life on this side of the world. The most popular item was an air mattress, like the kind you blow up and lay on in the pool, which was used to lay on top of your cot to act as a mattress. Some guys would even have sheets sent over to wrap around the air mattresses. Most guys just used their poncho covers as a blanket for the cool nights but some even had blankets sent over…whatever made you feel at home.

Of course, the main accessory in our hooch was the corner bar with our personalized supply of whiskeys, beers, and real glasses, not tin cups. Joe was usually the bartender and could make just about anything you ordered as long as it contained whiskey, scotch, bourbon, or water. This was about the only time you could drink water and not have to treat it first with a water purification tablet to kill the germs and scum in it, but at our bar the booze killed anything that was in there. Also, usually at the bar were any goodies from home that someone would get in the mail and set out for everyone to enjoy…cookies, cakes, candy, canned fruit, whatever came in one of our "care packages" from home. Everything that came in the mail to the guys was shared by all, from the homemade treats to the magazines to the music, everyone shared everything.

While sitting around drinking in my hooch one night, I was looking through some of the things that accumulated in my area when I ran across the net bag I had received at Christmas time. I had used most of the articles that the bag contained but inside was the note from Patty that I had never answered. So, I decided to drop her a line and thank her for her gift and say hello to a girl I didn't know. I didn't really know exactly what to write about, the war seemed like a very poor subject, so most of my letter was just a polite hello.

All of our mail was sent home to the states for free, so writing is something we all tried to do as often as possible. This was our gift from the government for being over here; we simply wrote the word FREE in the corner of the envelope where the stamp would normally be and off it went. I dropped off the letter to Patty and figured if she wrote back I'd probably here from her in about a week and a half, but I really didn't expect to hear from her at all. My feeling was that she took part in the company Christmas time function, but how many girls really had the time to write someone overseas, especially someone they didn't really know.

Well, surprise, surprise! Within a week along came a letter from Patty that not only was a polite hello but was about five pages long. I mean, first its taking the time to do it, then its knowing what to say and how to write what you want to say on paper; its more of a chore for people than it is a pleasure, so we only really do it when we have to. So why was she writing a five page letter to someone she didn't even know? Let's find out!

First of all, her handwriting was fascinating. Most girls have a really good handwriting, but hers was picture perfect. Each capital letter looked like old English script and each letter that followed was so smoothly formed. It really sounds stupid to harp on handwriting so much, but I had been criticized all throughout my life for having such good handwriting for a guy. The first thing everyone wanted to know is if I was a draftsman or printer, I guess I inherited it from my parents, I don't know!

Her letter was amazingly comfortable to read, seeing how I didn't know squat about her, and most of it told about her and her enjoyment in helping to put together packages for the guys overseas.

> *I'm nineteen years old, stand about five foot five inches, have brown hair, brown eyes, and weigh about one hundred fifteen pounds. I work full time at the Southern Bell Telephone Company as a telephone operator (yeah, I'm the one who sits there with the headset on like Ernestine alias Lily Tomlin). I live at home in Pensacola with my Aunt Jean and Uncle Sonny, my brothers Jeff and Mike, my niece Crystal, and our housekeeper Doretta. Jean is my salvation, no one understands me like Jean does!*

I had never personally known a girl from the deep South before and when you form impressions of the unknown, it usually is filled with fantasies of television dramas and movie scripts. The women, with long full flowing dresses and parasols twirling in the hot muggy southern sunlight, sitting on the veranda of a giant plantation; black servants waiting on them hand and foot, while fanning them with long handled bamboo fans. The talk is slow with a draw that stretches each sentence to a paragraph, and the mood is slow, lazy, and dominating, to the point of almost being snobbish.

This could not possibly be the way things are though, this is just an unreal picture painted in our minds by the pen of a Margaret Mitchell but to my surprise it is in some cases not far from reality.

We continued to write regularly and her first few letters brought me closely familiar with her lifestyle and environment.

> *Some of my favorite things are shopping (I buy anything and everything), reading (nothing like a good book to pass the day), music (I love Simon and Garfunkle and Peter, Paul & Mary...I hate classical!), and most of all the beach. You sound so much like me it's uncanny. I'm afraid of becoming a mean grouchy old lady that I want to stay young and happy just as long as possible. When I was thirteen I looked nineteen. I was so mature and reserved it was unbelievable. Now that I'm nineteen I tend to act like a kid. I like nothing better than pulling on a sweatshirt and tearing to the beach. The beach is a fab place!*

For many reasons our writing styles were so alike and we not only learned each other's ways but continually teased each other with lines that not only asked questions but answered them too. Our sense of humor was what dominated our styles the most, something I needed at a time like this. Before too long her letters were the highlight of my day.

> *Hi! Yes I know I just wrote you, it seems, but I couldn't wait to talk to you again. I'm sort of shy about writing to you so much, I guess. Seems all I want to do is write to you. (I've sadly neglected the poor ole college pals I used to write every week or so, doesn't that make you feel good!)*

Her letters were now arriving at almost a daily pace, and as tough as it was, I tried to keep up with her. Letter writing was no longer a chore but something I looked forward to and enjoyed. Mail call was now my favorite part of the day and as each letter arrived, I would savor the moment of reading it until the days duties were over and I could settle down with a drink and concentrate on what to convey to Patty.

Just think if we write this much now...think how much we'll talk. Gee, that's gonna be great! Well goodnight for now, I'll write ASAP (your terms are rubbing off on me!).

As the weeks went by, the war intensified more and more. Our artillery guns were getting a real workout each day and night and enemy activity in the area was growing at a quickening rate. Our daily duties increased to not only aerial plotting of infiltration routes, but foot patrols were formed each day and evening to set up ambush positions. Our enemy, the Communist-led forces, or Viet-Cong (viet for Vietnam, cong was short for cong-san meaning communist), were filtering into the area at an alarming rate. Our main job was to cut off their routes to the south throughout our area, but unfortunately they used the Ho Chi Minh Trail, through Laos and Cambodia, for the flow of their arms, ammunitions, and supplies. We, of course, couldn't touch them because we were not allowed to fire out of the country into Laos or Cambodia. Our war was not with them...it was crazy! Our guys in the field could be chasing or tracking a company of North Vietnamese Army (NVA) troops and as soon as we hit the Cambodian border, we had to stop! It was insane—was this war or a game of chess? The NVA had the advantage of hitting us anytime they wanted from wherever they wanted—we had to stay on our side of the line, no fair, not allowed to cross. Bullshit! I would finally get home from Nam, serve eight more months, get out of the service, grow two years older, and get married before our political leaders would finally come to their senses and go into Cambodia. But—too late!

On top of all of this, as the month of March approached we entered one of the monsoon seasons, which meant we had not only the enemy to fight but also Mother Nature was against us. Boy did it rain!

The downpour at times was so strong and forceful it rained horizontally instead of vertically. If it didn't rain all day, it usually rained several times a day. Before too long everything was wet! Everything we owned either went limp, stayed soaked, rotted, disintegrated, or mildewed so much it wasn't worth a damn. Even our skin stayed so wet we were walking prunes, so white and shriveled up.

As a reward for all the rain, we had gooey Vietnam mud to cling to us wherever we went. Grey ugly mud that oozed over, around, and through everything you came into contact with. The whole season just made life so pleasant to deal with!

THE REALITY OF WAR

On a warm still night in mid-March the reality of where we were was driven home by our fear of survival. At approximately two in the morning, we were awakened by the sound of enemy mortar fire that pierced the night air like a siren slicing the quiet of a lazy summer afternoon. After months of being a working part of an artillery unit, we had become accustomed to the continuous barrage of shells being fired throughout the night. Continuous explosions rip the short stillness of the night as long range enemy positions are pounded throughout the jungle, but the sound of incoming rounds awakens the mind and brings dancing dreams of fantasy to a sudden arousal of reality.

I immediately rolled out of my bedroll and scampered fiercely for my helmet and rifle as pandemonium shot throughout the tent. Screams of "incoming, incoming!" were echoing through my ears as panic replaced the calm of the night. We crawled to the outside bunkers which lined the sides of our hooches as the striking flashes of death encircled our camp. The first flash of light that I saw as I slithered out of the hooch broke the darkness like a flashbulb spraying your eyes with dots of light. It exploded on a Vietnamese tomb bringing to light the reality of death, past and present. We huddled inside our bunker as the cold mud floor made us shiver even more than we already were. Silence was broken by an occasional prayer as for the first time in Phu Bai we were the target and not the observer.

What seemed like two hours was over in ten minutes as we knew this was our signal to transform our months of practice into moments of defensive action. Like a piece of finely tuned machinery, each member had his duty to perform during what we knew would only be a few minutes of silence. My job was to run to the ammunition bunker, load up with straps of ammunition and boxes of grenades to be distributed to bunkers lining the perimeter of our compound. As I zigzagged through the hooches on my way to the ammo dump, the tension of the situation stiffened my body as constant thoughts of death surfaced in my mind. As I arrived at the bunker, ammunition was frantically being distributed to my fellow comrades who were as half-dressed and half-bewildered as I was. All of a sudden the strong rigid faces of manhood seemed to shatter into the scared nervous looks of a group of boys; boys who had trained so long to become men that their experience seemed to surpass their age.

I grabbed about ten bandoliers of M-16 ammo and two cases of hand grenades and was off and running to the northeast sector that my guys were at. Halfway between the ammo dump and my destination, the terror of war again entered my little corner of the world. I crashed to my stomach as the mortar fire resumed its unmerciful assault into our compound. The fright I had experienced before was but a fragment compared to the total fear I was surrounded by now. Not only was I now alone, but with no bunker as protection and ammo strapped to me high and low. I was a walking time-bomb!

I hugged the cold wet Vietnamese dirt and thought of hundreds of places I'd rather be. By the time I squirmed slowly across the ground to a nearby bunker, the shelling again stopped, and again all hell broke loose. I jumped to my feet and headed for the perimeter, much more confident that I would make it this time. As I ran a parallel path alongside our six bunkers, I tossed in straps of ammo and boxes of grenades until I reached the far hole which I swiftly jumped into.

Joe and Diff were already loading rifle clips for us to use should the frontal assault occur.

As quickly as the mortaring had stopped, guns started to explode with a deafening sound; but this time it was our guns firing illumination rounds into the sky to light up the area outside our perimeter. All eyes became intensely focused on the dimly lit perimeter searching for the slightest movement of enemy forces.

Our eyes were finally convinced that there was no frontal assault and we could relax a little bit. My eyesight focused on my two comrades firmly implanted in the foxhole next to me. Joe had a half-lit cigarette in one hand and replacing the usual can of beer in his other hand was his M-16 rifle poised and ready for action. Diff had the usual stump of a three day old cigar in the left side of his mouth and his yellow and black Maryland flag draped over his shoulders, a symbol of his personal feelings that you can put his body in Vietnam, but he will always have a little chunk of his homeland right there with him. We were all shirtless with flak jackets on and camouflaged helmets which seemed to give us all that GI Joe appearance that none of us cared to have.

Diff was the first to break the silence saying, "God damn gooks, of all nights to pick, they had to choose the one night that I finally got Mindy to the beach. We were just laying down on the sand when those damn mortars rolled me out of the sack."

"You gotta be kiddin' me," said Joe, "three friggin' months we been here and you haven't got in her pants yet?"

"Shit, Joe, we're only over in this godforsaken place for thirteen months, he'll have to re-enlist just to get her to the beach again." I said.

As the three of us laughed I could feel the tension of the situation slowly dissolve as we were all sure the worse part of our dramatic dilemma was over.

By now our artillery was starting to bombard the area where the enemy muzzle flashes had been spotted. Huey gunships were also visible as they flooded the sky with rounds of continuous fire power; bullets streaming down forming thin orange lines of brilliance as if to connect the sky with the ground. It took approximately twenty minutes for us to confidently realize that the enemy attack was subdued and we could stop staring at the perimeter which seemed to have a hypnotic hold on us.

I lit a cigarette and offered one to Joe and Diff, "Cigarette for a beer?"

"Sounds good to me," said Joe as he opened the flap of his trousers and threw me a San Miguel. "Would you believe this came out of the next to last case…if we don't make a beer run today it's gonna be awful dry around here this weekend!"

"I'll be damn if I'm gonna work around here with no alcohol for relaxation, I'll quit," snapped Diff.

"Well, we're supposed to make a beer run tomorrow so don't start gettin' withdrawal shakes. Anyway, we can always dip into our emergency private stock from the good ole real world," I said. "I've got two fifths left and I know Joe has at least a quart, right pal?"

Shhhh," whispered Joe, "you want Danson to hear you? That boozer would croak if he knew we had American whiskey and didn't tell him. He's been drinkin that shit from the gooks for three weeks now just prayin' that this month his monthly care package from home would come, but no luck yet."

"Yeah, I bet he's dying," laughed Diff, "now that we've moved, it'll take an extra two weeks before our mail catches up with us."

The shelling was starting to subdue as Sergeant Whitt came running down from bunker to bunker. The sky was still bright with illumination rounds as they whistled down from the sky leaving billowy trails of smoke lingering behind them.

"Everybody make it okay here?" asked Sgt. Whitt as he jumped into the bunker with us.

"Yeah, fantastic," I said. "Glad you could drop in!"

"Well, I was in the area so I thought, why not. Christ, I think I'd shit if I ever saw you three not drinkin' beer. How the hell can you drink at a time like this?"

"A time like what?" said Diff. "We come out here every night at three in the morning to relax and shoot the shit. Want a brew, Sarge?"

"No thanks, I'll take a Bloody Mary though!"

"Sorry, Sarge, wrong bunker. Mixed drinks are two holes down on the right!" snapped Diff as his laughter knocked the cigar stump out of his mouth.

"Nice job with the ammo G, see any casualties along the way?" asked Whitt.

"No, no personnel," I answered. "But I wouldn't give a whole lot of money for the right side of the mess hall right now!"

"Are you shittin' me, that's the kitchen side...we'll be on C-rations and powdered crap if the kitchens destroyed," shouted Joe.

"Well, on the last barrage I saw at least three mortar shells hit there so I know there's definitely some damage. Damn gooks – they couldn't hit the Vietnamese shops or even the motor pool, they gotta hit us right where it hurts...our stomachs!"

We each kind of drifted into our own little world for a while as we relaxed our minds and thought of places we'd rather be. My mind, of course, immediately shifted to Patty and how great it would be to be on the beach with her now, sitting in a different kind of sand than I was surrounded by here.

> *My friends and I went out tonight to a place called the Firehouse, a drive-in that used to be a fire station. We got some oyster boxes and cokes and then took our goodies down to the beach and ate. It was so dark it's a wonder we could see what we were eating. I kind of drifted off to the side by myself and sat on the rocks by the waters edge. My mind wandered to you and how nice it would be to have you here now, beside me. We both love the beach so much it just has to be our meeting place (I can see it now – as we run to each other from opposite sides of the beach, our arms open wide, running in slow motion. Then we meet, and embrace! Oh my...). I've got to stop wandering like this, what will my shrink say? Anyway...the beach it is!!*

After about an hour passed, we concluded that the attack on our camp had been merely a mortar assault and no ground forces would be threatening us. As the artillery guns continued to pound the area of the attack, illumination rounds would continue to light up the area for several hours to come. A small unit of men was assigned to patrol the area on the west and south perimeters in addition to the normal listening posts manned each night.

The rest of us headed back to camp to survey the damage which we feared was extensive to say the least. Our first instinct was to check out the mess hall which I feared was hit the worse. I was right, at least three mortar shells had crashed through the back half demolishing the kitchen and everything inside. Kitchen paraphernalia was thrown everywhere as the inside of the hall was simply made a part of the outside surroundings. The damage would definitely have us eating 'C' rations for at least a few days.

All in all we were very lucky, other than the mess hall only two hooches were damaged, two vehicles, and luckily no fatalities. Two guys had received minor shrapnel wounds but other than being shaken up a little, we were all in one piece...but totally pissed off!

> *All the news back here is Vietnam, Vietnam, Vietnam—it's really hard for me to cope with at times. When I try to forget where you are and what could happen to you, I pick up the newspaper or turn on the radio and I'm immediately reminded. You've really become a big part of my life, a part I think I was missing before (Jean always says it's what should be inside my head that's missing). When I was little I used to keep a diary, I'd write down every little thing I did, who was mean to me, what I thought of everybody; I finally got bored and stopped. At times this is like a diary to me, except it answers back, it has feelings and it cares (I hope). Take care...say hi to Joe.*

The next day was a busy one; everyone was feverishly working to restore our area back to the way it was before our Viet-Cong neighbors rearranged things. Lt. Barton grabbed Joe and I as soon as we walked out of the hooch in the morning and told us to get suited up for a patrol, we were going to investigate the nearest village just to our south for enemy activity. This village was the closest to our camp and was occupied by most of the Vietnamese that serviced our camp in one way or another, by servicing our camp they provided us with laundry service, gave us haircuts, sold us trinkets and souvenirs, and provided us with whiskey and women if that's what we needed. They were also paid to perform various jobs in the camp such as cleaning the area and burning with diesel fuel the big half-barrel drums that were used in our make-shift outhouses. All of these duties were performed proficiently while smiling and convincing us that they appreciated everything we were doing for them and they were our friends. This may be true, but when it came to our lives or theirs, they would side with the VC in a minute to save their own skin. It was for this reason that we wanted to canvas their village to find out if they knew of the attack on our base and to see if they harbored any of the enemy.

Our mission was a simple one—chopper in, search and disturb, chopper out!

It was a bright hot morning but moisture lay in the air which was unusual for a climate like this. It rains just about every day this time of year, with monsoons as much a part of the local environment as black pajamas and rice paddies; but with the intense tropical heat of the day, the rain just doesn't bother you at all. You can be soaking wet one minute and completely dry the next, as the hot climate of the day bakes the moisture out of your clothes.

Our squad consisted of twelve of us who were proficient in getting in, patrolling the area for suspected VC routes, and getting out, hopefully without bringing too much attention to ourselves. Our job as an artillery unit was much different from that of an infantry patrol unit, whose primary mission is to search and destroy; our mission is search and surveillance. The Viet-Cong are small, sneaky, conniving individuals who thrive on undetectable rodent-like habits to survive day to day. To infiltrate their area and become an undetected intruder is as difficult a task as trying to figure out why we as Americans are in this godforsaken terrain in the first place.

Our choppers were gassed up and ready as the bright sun pushed the first rays of the day through the treetop horizon. The stillness of the now quiet artillery guns was broken only by the whirling helicopter blades splitting the air at top speed.

We boarded the two choppers and made a smooth lofty takeoff over the treetops in a southerly direction. It was a smooth gliding ride as we raced over the dense jungle and vastly open rice paddies at what seemed like three hundred feet. We were moving at a much slower speed than we normally do when the lieutenant and I are out by ourselves; I guess the combination of weight, with six soldiers instead of two, and the extra cautiousness of the pilot was the reason.

As our short journey came to an end, we could see the small Vietnamese village sitting on the edge of a large clearing which we could use as our landing zone (LZ). We made several passes in all directions but could spot no movement in the village or surrounding areas. Our chopper hovered over the clearing and swiftly made its descent to the open field. I could feel the adrenalin flowing as we stood on the skids and began to jump out six feet before touchdown. We raced across the field in a crouched position, rifle ready, and eyes alert. As we hit the edge of the woods we fell to our knees swirling in the direction of the choppers to cover the remaining members of our squad. It seemed as if the chopper barely made it to the ground and away it went, leaving its cargo to the mercy of the area.

The lieutenant brought immediate organization to the squad as we huddled together like twelve newborn pups. We promptly set our minds to the task at hand which we had trained for so long to master. I immediately called on my radio to our artillery base, codename "Ladybug," to establish communication and acknowledge our successful infiltration of the area as the lieutenant studied his map aligning the coordinates of our environment in case artillery firepower was needed.

"Have you established contact with Ladybug yet G?" asked Lt. Barton.

"Yes, sir," I replied. "Ladybug has us loud and clear and is standing by for further orders. They have a full battery pointed our way. I also have 'Snoopy' standing by just waiting for the word."

Snoopy was the name given to the Huey gunship supporting us on patrol should we need immediate air support.

"Okay, G, sounds good, now let's get this shittin' patrol on the move, we don't want to sit in one spot too long."

We started in towards the village which was about one hundred yards from the edge of the clearing we had landed in. From the air we had seen that the village looked deserted and it was obvious from our location that the area had not been inhabited in quite some time. As we drew closer to the outskirts of the village a faint stench filled the air; a stench that usually accompanies the Vietnamese peasant people.

"Smells like there's been some activity around here," remarked Diff.

"Yeah, either the gooks have been through here or somebody farted," whispered Joe.

The area had grown immensely quiet since the sounds of the choppers had all but disappeared. We had spread out in a wide column and began to sweep through the area examining every nook and cranny of the terrain for telltale signs of enemy as well as friendly activity. It was a known fact that the friendly inhabitants of a village will leave when Viet-Cong are in the area, but return as soon as they have left. The Vietnamese people were insanely afraid of the VC mainly because of the animalistic nature the Cong practiced. To make sure the villagers would not help the Americans or give away the VC positions, the VC would sneak into a village late at night, capture one of their prominent citizens or young females, and completely mutilate or rape them for the entire village to see; a barbaric and inhumane action, but normal and fun-seeking for these uncivilized soldiers, who slept by day and lurked by night. The Americans controlled the daylight but the nighttime belonged to the VC. Charlie, as they were called by us, knew this land like the back of their hand and if he couldn't evade you above the ground, he'd definitely evade you below the ground in his amazing system of tunnels; holes in the ground that led to underground systems and supply routes, to other villages and camps, or to excruciating pain and suffering if they were traps for spirited Americans to fall into. Cold, dark holes in the ground, barely big enough for a small man's body to squeeze through, but waiting to be conquered or destroyed as if by invitation only. Many times these holes were booby-trapped with fine strands of wire that, when engaged, would throw a bouncing betty mine up waist high and blow your groin completely out. Entrances that would conceal a dungeon below that would fall through to a floor of sharp spiked bamboo spears dipped in poison or human defecation, just waiting for a human body to fall to its death upon them. The job of the American soldier was to investigate these passages and destroy them before they destroyed us or maimed us, a job that was a nightmare by day.

The lieutenant and I were in the middle of the column with five guys on each side of us, Diff and Joe were to my right while Ron, Lenny, and Mike were to my left. Everyone had his M-16 up and ready while Lt. Barton and I carried both M-16's and 45 caliber pistols.

As each of us advanced into the edge of the village, each step we took was careful and suspicious. We knew if Charlie had been in the area he would leave booby-traps strategically placed throughout the area just waiting for an unsuspecting soldier to experience its pain and destruction.

Each step I took was like moving my legs in slow motion yet even the light-footedness of my boots stirred up the dust of this hot, dry wasteland engulfing them with a residue of land itself. This was not a climate that normally brought sweat to the brow, but the live intensity of the situation brought streams of perspiration rolling down the cheeks of my face.

Our eyes were darting fiercely between the ground where we walked and the foreign village which lay waiting only a few yards in front of us. The weak grass shanties with bamboo and thatch roofs, stood still as if focused for a picture postcard with neither a breeze nor intruder to ruin its scenic content.

It looked to be a total of eight huts in the hamlet, three on each side with two centered, as if protected by the rest. We split up into three groups to sweep through the huts, with the lieutenant and I taking the center huts and the other two groups of five covering each side of three huts.

"Be careful and watch out for anything that may be booby-trapped," said Lt. Barton as the squad split apart.

We approached the first center hut cautiously, crouching as we slowly ran, one to each side of the entrance. I knelt down momentarily to readjust the radio strapped to my back and to make sure the volume and squelch controls were turned down, just barely on. I gave the lieutenant the thumbs up that I was ready to go and we proceeded to slowly walk towards the doorway leading into the hut. Our movements seemed to be in a slow motion state as we neared the entrance and burst in, one high and one low. The hut was empty except for a smattering of personal belongings scattered here and there. A makeshift chair was in one corner while in the other stood a tall wooden box with a water basin on top. Beside the basin was a bar of soap and a razor, on the side were two rags hanging from a rusty nail. As I gazed around the hut I could not imagine this being 'home' to someone. Two piles of tall cut grass were spread on one side to form what must have been the bed, with two hand-made pillows made of some kind of animal hide lying near the top.

"Home sweet home," I said as I turned with the lieutenant to leave.

"Let's hit the other one then wait for the guys back at the clearing."

We walked out and headed towards the second hut located about twenty yards behind the first. As we reached the entrance and started in, a loud explosion rang throughout the area involuntarily knocking us to the ground. We rolled over glancing in the direction of the explosion and saw the side blown out of one of the huts on the left side. The upper half of the grass and mud wall was completely blown out down to a little make-shift window, as well as one-fourth of the roof attached above it.

Screams could be heard from inside the hut as we crawled to the side of a bush lining the pathway. Two of our guys were moving to run in when out of the doorway staggered Mike. His face and arms were splattered with blood as his rifle drug the ground behind him.

I grabbed the handset on my radio and made contact with Ladybug and Snoopy. The lieutenant jumped up and ran towards Mike and the others yelling for a status of what was going on.

"A grenade," cried Mike, "a goddamn live grenade!"

By now all of the guys were in the area and I was sure that there was no confrontation from the explosion; the village was definitely barren of life.

"Snoopy, this is X-ray patrol, need med-evac assistance now. Area is secure, I repeat, area is secure, no Victor Charlie in sight. Request dust-off, over." I had panic in my voice as I pleaded for help.

"X-ray, this is Snoopy, read you loud and clear, estimated ETA 45 seconds. How many casualties, over?"

"This is X-ray, wait one." I ran over to where our guys were huddled in a circle near the entrance of the hut.

"How bad is it?" I asked. "Snoopy is comin' in for a med-evac."

"Two bad." said the lieutenant. "Mike is pretty stunned and peppered with shrapnel, but he'll be okay for now. We'll get the others in the chopper first and on the way, Mike can go back on the second chopper."

I looked over and could see Bill and Eddie lying in a pool of blood. Eddie's hand and half his arm were blown away with just strings of flesh hanging at the elbow; his head was so covered in red that I couldn't tell if I was looking at the outside of his head or inside. He was alive and conscious, but definitely in shock as Diff tied a tourniquet around his upper arm to stop the bleeding. Bill was peppered with shrapnel wounds everywhere and I could see chunks of flesh dug out of his upper body and face.

"Snoopy, this is X-ray, two immediate casualties on the way. Starting to transport now, over."

The immediate answer from the Huey was loud and clear as I glanced over in the clearing and could see the chopper slowly descending. "Roger, X-ray, we're waiting on you."

Panic-stricken was the only word to describe Bill as he screamed and cried nonstop. "Help me, help me, I'm gonna' die. Oh my god look at me! Mom? Mom, where are you?"

It was obvious that they both needed attention quick. Diff, Joe, and Lt. Barton were working feverishly to dress the wounds as the other guys lifted Eddie and Bill for the short run to the chopper. A few of the other guys had spread out to watch the area in case any VC heard the explosion or saw the chopper coming in.

The dust stirred up by the chopper was like a windstorm as it covered everything in sight. Covers were thrown over the two stretchers as they approached the choppers to keep the wounds as clean as possible. Within seconds the Huey was airborne, its huge rockets and guns idled by the emergency of the situation at hand.

"X-ray, this is Ladybug, come in, over," echoed my radio as the noise of the chopper drifted in the distance.

"This is X-ray, go ahead," I answered.

"Roger, X-ray, request situation status, over."

"Tell them to pick us up ASAP and have medical attention ready for Mike," said the lieutenant as he wiped the blood from his hands.

I answered the call and unloaded the radio off my back as I fell to my knees. We all huddled at the edge of the clearing under a large out-of-place tree, each trying to reconstruct in our minds what had just happened.

"Mike," asked the Lieutenant, "feel like talking?"

"Sure," answered Mike as he sat shivering on a large rock sticking out of the ground. "Eddie and Bill went in the hut first and saw there was no one inside, they motioned to Lenny and I that it was all clear. As I walked in the doorway ahead of Lenny, Bill was just pushing aside a GI helmet with the tip of his rifle. I yelled no, stop, but all of a sudden from underneath the helmet a hand-grenade rolled out, fell off the box onto the floor, armed and ready. In an instant, Eddie pushed Bill aside, grabbed the live grenade, and was in the motion of tossing it out the small window when it went off. Eddie and Bill took the brunt of the impact; I just caught a lot of shrapnel that had gone through them. God it was just so quick! I yelled for him to stop moving the helmet, but it was too late."

Mike continued to shake and shiver as he told us his story. His face and arms were dotted with red circles and cuts that made him appear to have a bad case of the measles. Ron, who was sitting beside him, began to soak a handkerchief with water and wipe Mike's brow. He knew Mike was lucky that he didn't take any of the initial blast, especially in the face and eyes.

"Damn gooks. Did you see the look in Eddie's eyes? I sure as hell hope he makes it," said Mike as he put his head in his hands, "he shouldn't have been going in first, he's too green, he's only been over here two months. I should have been going in, I know better than to touch anything. Damn it!"

"Take it easy, Mike; don't go blaming yourself, he should have known better. We get it pounded into our heads a thousand times not to touch anything. It's not your fault, those damn gooks knew we were coming," said Joe as he threw half a cup of water into the bushes. "They just set that helmet up there propped on the pulled pin just waitin' for someone to move it. I hate this frigin' war!"

Tears rolled down his eyes as he kicked the dirt and lit yet another cigarette.

"Gimme' one," I said as I punched him on the arm throwing him off balance. "Take it easy, pal."

"I'm okay," he said, "just pissed off that's all!"

We were all pissed off. This whole thing was just wrong. What in the hell were we doing here?

For the longest time all of us sat in silence searching for the reason behind all of the insanity. Only the swirling sounds of chopper blades brought us back to reality as we gathered our thoughts and proceeded to our pickup point.

Before long we were back at base recalling the incidents of the day and trying to wash it all away with the medication of alcohol. Later that evening the word came down to us that both Eddie and Bill survived their ordeal and were resting comfortably in the hospital unit. Eddie would lose his entire right arm and facial damage was extensive enough that both his sight and hearing would be lost on one side. Bill was luckier; skin grafts would probably repair most of the damage to him, although he was not responding to sounds at all. The doctors felt his hearing may improve; the initial blast may have deadened his ear drums temporarily.

We all had a drink for them and prayed for their recovery. We probably would never see them again; they would be sent home to stateside military hospitals to recover as soon as they were transportable. They could divorce themselves of this long unmerciful war, but the lasting and permanent effects from it would unfortunately live with them forever. God bless them!

As we finally made our way to our hooches, I saw the telltale sign that mail call had not passed me by. My day would at least END in peace.

> *G, I'm lonely, I miss you, and I want to talk to you – do you have time to listen to me? You're the one person I can always count on to be there when I have something to say. I can't wait to get another of your fab letters!*

A long painful day dealing with the reality of war…but peace at last!

MAIL CALL

Mail was everything; our life, our link to civilization. Each night that we weren't on watch or patrol it was as routine as the setting sun as each guy would settle down in his little corner and read over the letters he received that day. This was a time of joy if you got mail, or a time of emptiness if you didn't. We shared our mail with each other, in the sense that we all knew what was happening in each others' lives. The topic around the beer hooch each night was usually talk of home, of family, of sweethearts. We were part of each others lives, a part of the dreams, the happiness, and sometimes the sorrow. The only bad mail was the occasional *Dear John* letter that would arrive, shattering the hopes of many a guy when he needed the exact opposite. It was settling down at that peaceful time of the day with your daily reward, a letter from your sweetheart—only to read those dreaded words you had feared one day would come. The sudden shock of those few lines of print transforms your daily reward to a fearful reality. You travel with fears every hour of every day as you push through the jungle watching for that first flash of the enemy AK-47 that means a bullet is racing towards you, or the snap of a wire that triggers a booby-trap crippling your body. All the joy and laughter that usually surrounded a letter from your girl is missing, and the feeling is immediately picked up by everyone around you. It was time to be left alone. A time to read and re-read the miserable news that you hoped would never arrive. These letters not only affected the guy who got them, but the entire unit felt the pain and hurt, as if everyone in the unit had received a *Dear John*. It was a time for comradery and understanding. We were alone in a land far away from home. A land that didn't really care about us, only the result they hoped we would bring to their lives. If we didn't get mail, we felt forgotten by our country, forgotten by the land that had sent us to this hell hole. To quell those feelings we had each other, so what would affect one of us, affected all of us. We were a unit.

There were times when I wondered if Patty's letters would dwindle off. She was young and exciting and certainly had more to do than sit home writing letters every night, but it seemed I was always wrong. Her letters not only continued but came more and more regularly.

> *Today was the pits at work, my boss got on my nerves, my friends got on my nerves, I even got on my own nerves! The traffic on the way home was awful and the heat was unbearable, but then I was greeted by a letter from you. What a way to bring me out of an awful day...you can't imagine how much I need you....*

It always amazed me that her mood was conveyed so easily in her letters. Even more amazing was that her mood was always so positive, so happy, so predictable. Even if her letter started out on a negative note or she was 'down' for some reason, by the second page she was her same old self. She often said she could pull herself out of the dumps by writing me a four or five page letter. I guess it was like she said before; almost like pouring your thoughts out to a diary except this diary had feelings and eventually answered back.

As each letter was exchanged we became infatuated with each other and began to grow increasingly close.

> *Sometimes I go out to Scenic Highway, it overlooks the Bay with it's quiet serenity. I just sit on the bluffs and think about you, about us. What we have to say to each other, what we are to each other, why I need you now. Great.... You're going through hell and I need you...*

Mail call made my day or shoved me back into the reality of this deprived situation. I usually got mail just about every day except when we would pull up camp and move to another area. This usually delayed our mail by a week or two, depending on where we moved. The areas we would move to were usually fairly secure since it was tough to move an artillery unit into an area that was not fully built up. So, with the size of our artillery forces we generally stayed up north, from supporting the DMZ at Dong Ha to supporting the areas around Hue and Phu Bai.

If I didn't get a letter from Patty, I'd usually get one from my parents, relatives, or one of the girls back home. It was always great to hear from my parents and one of them would try to write at least every other day. For them every day was a month long. Each day brought them more hope that the day would come when they no longer rushed to the mailbox every morning to see if a letter had arrived. The day that I would return home and their fears of the 'worst' would no longer come to mind. They truly spent thirteen months in Nam also! I always loved when I got a letter from them, it made me feel like I was home with them again…just for that moment.

The girls back home would try to write every week or so but their letters just weren't as exciting or stimulating as a letter from Patty or my parents. I guess when you get away from home in a situation like 'the service' you really lose the close ties you have with your friends at home, especially the girls. As much as they tell you that they'll be true-blue and wait for you to return, you really know deep down inside that for a teenage girl to take herself out of circulation with the world during the most 'fun' time of her life is ridiculous. Granted, some couples do remain true-blue to each other through this kind of ordeal, but the odds certainly are in favor of the masses that don't remain intact. And really it's only fair that you should separate for that time period and enjoy life and what's happening around you. If the two of you were meant for each other then your separation will survive and she'll be waiting for you to return.

I had been dating one girl for a long time, since I was fifteen, and when I left for the Marine Corp at eighteen she vowed to wait until the ends of time. Bullshit! I really knew Ashley and I were going our separate ways far before the USMC came into my life. I really believe we had been together too long and had really grown apart from each other as each day progressed.

Anyway it was great to hear from Ashley, even though they were all lies. The one girl I really did enjoy hearing from was Diane. She was the first real girlfriend I had when I was about thirteen years old. She lived in back of us and I really believe we hit it off from the first time we looked each other's way. She was always a pretty girl, petite, with short auburn hair and a smile that would light up even the cloudiest day. My one big regret in life is the way I treated our relationship through the years.

As we grew older I took her for granted on so many occasions, and when it came down to her or someone else, I always went the other way. Why? She was the kind of girl any guy would love to have, and once I went away in the service she found herself a nice guy and eventually married him. I lost contact with her, but truly hope has had everything coming to her in life. While I was in the service, she would write and at times we would talk about the love we had lost; her letters brought sad memories to me, but I really enjoyed hearing from her.

Those were probably the two most important girls in my life prior to the Marine Corps, but since shipping overseas, Patty had become my one true friend. Patty's letters were special. I guess it was the closeness the two of us built around each other. A friendship built on the relationship of two strangers relying on each other to pull them through some difficult times. My situation over here in Nam was obvious, but Patty also had a need that had to be fulfilled. I was her escape from the everyday hustle and bustle of Pensacola, Florida, and someone she could talk to and confide in. A friend.

She kept me fairly well apprised of her social life and was basically more of a down-home shy type person, although given the right situation and escort, she wasn't afraid to let her hair down and go just a little crazy. Many times we talked over her adventures and at the same time made plans for ours. Our adventure was sometimes easy to talk about, but how easily could a relationship we had developed by words, be replaced by a true to life relationship? Feelings are expressed very easily through the written letter or over the phone, but sometimes it serves only as a crutch. The reality of losing that crutch and meeting face to face is a reality not easily confronted by many people, but one we would dream about for over a year. As she hit obstacles in her everyday life she would spend an hour or two with me and talk over her problems.

> *Your letter today brightened what was one of the worse days I have had in a while. I'm so glad we have each other to do all this mutual day-brightening. Even when I get a chance to write twice in one day I still feel sad that I don't have more time to spend with you.*

One of the continuing requests that she would have was she wanted to do something for me.

> *I want to send you something, give you something, help you in some way...I feel helpless, all I do is write, I want to do more!*

Here she was giving me the very thing I needed most, companionship, the will to continue, and the hope that one day I would not only write to Patty, I would talk to Patty in person. I would return from Nam in one piece and I would live to see my dream come true. And she wanted to do more—something meaningful!

I did have one big request of her though, I wanted a picture. I not only wanted to talk to her via the pen, I wanted to gaze into her eyes and see this beautiful person that was part of me now. Many times throughout the months of the summer I would ask for that ultimate gift and most of the time she would acknowledge the request and go on.

But finally….

> *I am going to send you a picture, I promise. I'll make an appointment to have a good one taken next week. If you only knew what a traumatic experience pictures are for me! I really do have a photo-phobia! But I promise, a picture (or flick as you GI's call it) will soon be on the way. But I want a snapshot of you too, Gary. I'd like to 'see' you when I write. Life magazine did an article on Vietnam last week, and one picture was of a couple of guys on a tank. The one on the right was blonde and wearing a pair of cool sunglasses. I think he had a headset around his neck and that's what really reminded me of you. I don't know that you even where a headset! Maybe you don't. Oh you do, okay! Anyway, 'that looks like Gary' kept breezing through my mind.*

Her words encouraged me and made me continue. She never mentioned war and fighting, I'm not sure whether that was on purpose or not, but everything she wrote seemed to entice you to "*wait and see what tomorrow will bring.*" This is truly the encouragement that we needed in Vietnam, the desire to continue and arrive at the next day with a will to continue. Men in the armed forces need to hear the sound of their name echoing at mail call; it is a time in their lives that they are away from everything they really care about. But for the servicemen fighting overseas in a war that isn't theirs, they need to not only hear from the people at home but to receive the words of encouragement that will get them into the next day of life. It is so easy just to give up and say the hell with it; it is so easy to believe that you've been forgotten and left to fight a war nobody wants or cares about. The service has drilled your service ID number into your head for so long you forget that you are really a person, a human being who is cared about. It was tough for all of us, and we didn't even have it as bad as our fellow warriors did in the two

World Wars they fought. They went into war until it was finished if they were lucky enough to last that long…we were only sent into hell for thirteen months. The government felt that if they instituted a mandatory rotation of its men it would be easier to keep up morale within the troops, it would give the troops a goal to shoot for, an end would always be in sight. The problem was they forgot the guarantee that you'd make it through thirteen months to finish your tour and they forgot that morale is build through daily will and encouragement, not just time.

Vietnam was a hell on earth. A war being fought by teenagers, in a land they had never heard of, for a cause they couldn't explain. A war that had no front lines, no humane ethics, and no American support…a war nobody wanted but a war we were told to fight!

The days grew longer and the patrols and the shelling seemed endless. Each new day seemed to re-create the day before which led to boredom, restlessness, and low morale. The times we went out on patrol, if our spirit was down, then so was our sharpness. If it's one thing you don't need it's an uncaring attitude when you are out in the bush. One careless mistake can cost the whole squad their life. You needed to depend on each other to not only protect both your sides, but to keep each other 'up' and ready. No easy task in the barren wastelands of hell.

> *Time is really passing by (I'm sure I'm telling you something you don't already know), I can't believe another month has gone by. Before you know it G, you'll be here in the World (as you GI's call it), and I'm sure the girls will be waiting. There are a lot of lonely females back here waiting for some real men to sweep them off their feet….*

Way to go, Patty, what a way to boost the morale. Her timing was always remarkable.

Before too long, I was over halfway through my tour of duty, in fact, I was almost two-thirds through my entire Marine Corp hitch. I would only have eight months left in the service when I got back to the states, that's unless I re-enlist for a couple more years! Anyone would have to be insane to stay in the service longer than absolutely necessary. It takes a certain kind of person to give up the freedom of life and the pursuit of happiness to serve for Uncle Sam longer than the minimum. I was stupid enough to voluntarily enlist in the first place; I certainly wasn't going to commit a far worse act of insanity by 're-uping' for more.

I occasionally heard from my 'buddy' Stan, who got me into this whole mess. He was also in Nam and positioned north of us in Con Thien with a tank unit. While I had gone to San Diego to the radio school for training, Stan was sent to armored vehicle school to learn the ins and outs of the war on wheels. He too was counting the days until our tour was up, and of course he blamed 'me' for everything!

About every third or fourth night I would pull night watch out on one of the listening posts (LP) that encircled the compound. A couple of the outposts were wooden towers that stood about twenty-five feet high and had enough room in the covered platform on top for one or two men, a lawn chair, and a 50-caliber machine gun set-up. The other outposts were just ground level bunkers, usually about three sandbags deep and big enough to hold half a dozen men or so. Each bunker was equipped with a radio, a set of binoculars, and all the instruments needed to destroy life, should a ground attack occur. Oh boy!

Each post also had a starlight scope which helped immensely as the sun would sink below the horizon taking with it your one sense of security, your ability to see what was happening in front of you. The single ocular device used the light from the stars and moon to enlighten the projected view. It increased your night vision capability by lending a lightened green glow to the surrounding darkness.

This type of watch was pure hell, as the many tricks of the night played deceiving little games with your eyes and your mind. The stillness of the calm warm night created strange unknown sounds that tempted the imagination with thoughts of enemy footsteps tiptoeing in the area right next to you. The darkness that filled the night was so black you found yourself touching your eyes to make sure they were really open. As your eyes adjusted to the moonlight, the shapes and shadows of each bush and tree came to life and danced a little closer with each tick of the clock. An outline that wasn't there a minute ago, is now kneeling down, sneaking up on you as his comrades encircle your bunker for the surprise attack. Your stomach is tied in a knot as you can see them moving ever so cautiously, you can hear them walking ever so lightly, you can imagine that they are whispering and signaling their next move—but you know it's your imagination…or do you?

Your only recourse is to light up yet another cigarette and try not to stare so hard at the night-life around you; try not to listen so intently to the sounds of the night stillness. Maybe if you ignore them they'll go away! You certainly don't want to fire at them because killing trees and bushes is hard to explain as the entire camp is awakened and running to your rescue.

But for four long hours you play the game. At the end of your watch you've emptied a pack of cigarettes, and collected your thoughts so many times your head is pounding from the mental exercise of the night. Your only companion for the night has been your radio partner at the other end, who was glad he had you to keep him awake also!

It was usually a time spent thinking about what was happening in your life, and questioning if you'd make it to the end of your tour. This was the time I'd think most of Patty and what was going on in her life, and if we'd ever really meet. Each letter I'd receive from her brought more and more desire into my will to live and pull through this uncivilized, meaningless disgusting war. The time I'd spend with her helped me to forget where I was and why I was there. Her letters never questioned *if* I would come to see her only that the day was approaching *when* I would. She brought sanity and hope into a world that was barbaric to each person thrust into it. I just couldn't imagine a soldier over here who had no 'Patty' to lean on, no person like her to ensure you that life will go on and giving up was a phrase not to be uttered.

My war was mild compared to the war confronted by the grunts in the field every day; the men who actually met the VC face to face and fought for the little hill or piece of ground that meant nothing to either one of them personally. I had no desire to change places with them, the security of my artillery unit was a blanket I was glad to have wrapped around me, and the one I knew most grunts would love to have. For this reason alone, our support to the field was our utmost priority, our foremost concern, and our daily battle. If we could bring in artillery support to one trapped unit of men, or blow up one enemy supply route, or eliminate one VC ambush patrol, then we were doing our part to make their life a little easier. Our tour of duty was far more easier than theirs, but hopefully our contribution as a support unit would help to bring a lot more of our guys safely home.

Death is not rewarding. But the sheer pleasure of doing your 'job,' a job that saves the lives of your fellow soldiers, is a reward. The job of an artillery unit is to support the troops in the field and deter enemy forces from coming into the area. One such deterrent is death. As the radio operator for my unit, the lieutenant and I spent a good deal of our time not only flying over the area and plotting positions to be hit by our artillery during the night, but to lead patrols throughout the area in search of enemy activity. These patrols usually lead us to the high ground where we could observe any large enemy movements that may have been reported by our recon units in the area. Spotting enemy movement, especially large units, was the highlight of our day. Many times I'd even have trouble calling in the coordinates on the radio; the excitement of an enemy kill really pumped the adrenaline. As we confirmed and re-confirmed the location, our final command of "Fire!" would send a spotter shell exploding in the area. This round was usually a WP, or Willie Peter round, which exploded a white phosphorous chemical in all directions upon impact. Upon contact it literally burned anything in its path, clothing, flesh, anything. Once observing where the round hit, we would make any coordinate adjustments necessary, and give the command "Fire For Effect!" which would send a volley of HE, or High-Explosive, rounds down on the enemy units. When everything went right, it was a perfectly timed performance of team effort, from beginning to end. The results were usually dramatic. The WP rounds usually caught them by surprise and sent them scattering like a swarm of ants. The following rounds peppered the entire area so thoroughly; we could usually give a confirmed death count without too much investigation. It was fulfilling! Not the taking of human life, but the thought that maybe the elimination of this unit may save one of ours and bring us closer to the end. Death was never pretty, but many times fulfilling.

> *Most of the guys I know are in college and haven't had to go into the service yet, so you're really my only contact with that part of the world. I know there are a lot places you'd rather be right now, but unfortunately you had no choice, you were handed your orders and off you went. But all of you guys over there are doing a job that I guess has to be done. Each one of you is to be commended and we love you all. Please hurry home...*

The crutches of war were easy for some to accept but much harder on the guys who didn't have the 'Patty's' of the world to lean on. Smoking and drinking were of course the most prevalent habits that confronted our daily life, but more and more drugs were making their way into our reach as each month passed. When my tour of duty started it was rare that someone would even offer a 'joint' of marijuana during one of our all night patrols or even during our 'party-times.' But as the months went by some guys turned to that as a crutch that supported them during the rough times, the way Patty supported me. There were occasions when we all needed some artificial encouragement, but for Joe, Diff, and I it was more for the excitement of trial rather than the will of survival. By the end of our tour we would see many guys strung out on dependencies that would follow them home and become crutches throughout their day to day life. It was so easy to get things from the Vietnamese, who peddled everything from booze to cigarettes, to dope to girls; whatever you needed, they had. In my whole thirteen ugly months, I can only remember seeing one guy totally blown away by drugs; but I really think he brought his dependency over to Nam with him; he needed help from day one. He was the one person who never went on patrols or watch because he couldn't be trusted. I certainly wouldn't want him next to me during a firefight; I couldn't be sure what planet he'd be on! And I certainly wasn't going to sleep very well knowing he was keeping watch over the compound, I'd rather pull a double watch myself. For the most part everyone else knew their limits and knew when and how to pace themselves. You certainly had to think of more than yourself when you 'needed a drink'; the lives of too many people in camp, as well as in the field, are in your hands.

Patty and I talked a lot about these crutches people needed. She didn't understand why people needed these 'foreign' vices to get them by the daily routines of life, yet she seemed to understand how a soldier away from 'everything' may need some substitute to help cope.

Drinking had always been a part of my teenage life, but I considered myself a "social drinker" not a "dependant drinker."

> *That's okay! You can like a drink (not 'to drink') if you want to. I like a man who drinks a little. I also like a man who's both gentle and masculine. Appreciates fine art, fine music, and fine women, yet isn't too carried away with it all. Drinking is sort of an art too...like being a good conversationalist and a likable person, like you. Maybe you can teach me the fine art of social drinking when you come home. But you'll have to watch me...too much firewater may lead me astray...*

Why was she doing this to me? Was she trying to drive me crazy or what?

I think she knew what she was doing !!

A PABST BLUE RIBBON DAY

I spent the night recovering from those 'inviting' and tantalizing words; I was awakened in the morning to the sounds of Joe storming into the hooch shaking me and everything else in sight.

"Hey, G, rise and shine, we got an important mission to go on. Top Secret! Only the most qualified guys were chosen to go on this one!"

"What the hell are you talking about, Joe? This better be worth getting me up. I had LP watch last night, ya know!"

"Yeah, I know, but this is a mission I knew you wouldn't want to miss. C'mon, get up!" Joe said as he threw my hat and clothes on my rack.

"Okay, okay, I give up. What's this urgent mission that's beckoning us so early in the morning?"

"Diff, Ron, Mo, you, and I are making a run down to DaNang today to pick up supplies," snapped Joe with a shit-eatin' grin on his face.

"You got me out of the sack this early to make a goddamn supply run to DaNang? Are you crazy, Scalia?"

"Hey, G," he smirked as he burst from the seams laughing. "We're making a run to pick up six hundred cases of beer, American beer. A booze run man, a booze run!" He stood back with his arms spread wide open, "Hey, man, did I do good or what?"

With our destination and orders in hand, the four of us, Joe, Diff, Ron, and myself, piled into the six-by, while Mo hopped into the radio jeep to act as our escort, and away we went. Diff decided to drive first, since he was the senior ranking member of the group, and I rode shotgun, while Joe and Ron rode in the back bed of the empty truck.

"Well, this is one supply run I don't mind taking," said Diff as we rode through the entrance to the compound leaving a trail of dust that rose in the morning heat like a storm cloud engulfing the sky.

"No, but I'll be glad when we're pullin' back into the compound with all that beer in the back. It'll be great to pop a can of good beer for a change," I said as we hit the road to DaNang.

"Good beer? Did Danson tell you what kind it was…all I heard was how much?"

"Yeah, he said four hundred cases of Pabst Blue Ribbon from stateside and two hundred and fifty cases of San Miguel from the islands."

"Holy shit, four hundred cases of Pabst. I can't believe it! I used to think Pabst was real rot-gut beer, but now it sounds like Lowenbrau to my ears."

"You can say that again," shouted Joe from the back bed of the truck.

"Holy shit, four hundred cases of Pabst, I can't believe…"

"Aw suck ass!" interrupted Joe. "Just keep those shifty little eyes of yours on the damn road. If you get my young ass blown up by a land mine, there's gonna be a shit load of pissed off females back in the states for you to answer to!"

"You just keep your Italian ass ready in case we get hit and I'll get us over these damn pot-holed dirt roads." Diff had that reassuring tone in his voice. He made a believer out of you whether you were scared to death or not.

The roads were congested with the hustle of Vietnamese people tending to their everyday activities. Women and girls raced alongside the narrow one-vehicle road carrying fruits and vegetables in large wire-molded baskets that were either balanced on their head or from a long pole that was neatly centered on their shoulders. They were each dressed the same; long, black, shiny, loose-fitting silk material which hung low and baggy resembling pajamas more than clothing. Each had on a black, long, pointed hat that shaded their hard, strong, war-torn faces from the sweltering sun. Faces that were as dry and hard as the soil they worked in, each with occasional smiles that showed blackened stained teeth from chewing betel nut, which all women seemed to enjoy. As they walked at a running pace, concerned not with us or their surroundings, but only with their immediate job at hand, they seemed almost regimented to me. It was almost as if their country had been in a war for so long that the people dressed in the uniform-of-the-day and paraded hastily around at a pace that would soon get them under the safety of cover.

Weaving in and out of the pedestrian traffic were the ever-present Vietnamese children on their dilapidated make-shift bicycles. Their bright smiling faces showed the only happiness that this devastated land seemed to know. Faces of excitement, but faces that sat on a smallish framed body, crying for nutrition that would bring growth and strength to their weak frames. As we passed through each small village, their feet would pedal at a frantic pace to keep up with our truck while their hands and mouths never stopped for a second.

"Cigarette, Joe! Cigarette! Candy!"

It was always the same wherever we went; hungry kids yelling for cigarettes and candy as their hands were reaching and grasping at the empty air. Screaming to every GI that went by, calling him "Joe," which fulfilled the G.I. Joe image that all kids have for US Marines. It seemed as if everywhere you went in this jungle ridden country you were besieged with requests for candy or cigarettes, along with offers of American whiskey or women, which they all referred to as "my sister."

"Hey, Joe, you like to meet my sister, she show you good boom-boom (sex), she real clean, do it all!" yelled the kids as they desperately tried to keep up with our two-vehicle convoy. It always seemed like they knew exactly what was a priority to the strange homesick men invading their land...whiskey, women, and cigarettes. Of course, most of these kids had spent all of their lives seeing soldiers traveling the streets and fields; war was as much a part of their lives as poverty and starvation.

The biggest pain in the ass when driving the main routes through these villages was by far the Vietnamese drivers. Every vehicle you would see, which was very few, was an old jalopy or antique bus that had so many people hanging out of it that it was ridiculous. A small bus that held thirty people was loaded down with fifty or sixty bodies hanging out of the doors and windows, clinging to the front and rear bumpers, and laying on the roof as if their total survival depended on this one trip. Between the ridiculous width of these pot-holed roads, the people-laden buses, the kids on bicycles, and the women lining the edges of the routes, how could you possibly take your eyes off of the road?

I glanced to the back of the truck and was not surprised at all to see Ron partaking of his favorite pastime which was making the kids happy. No matter where our travels took us in Nam, Ron's large oversized jacket and pants pockets were overloaded with candy and goodies for the kids who would pedal their hearts out to keep up with the truck; all in hopes of catching just one piece of candy from the GI's. The smiles on the faces of these kids were only over-shadowed by the gigantic smile on Ron's face as he reached in his pockets and tossed handfuls of Mary Janes, Bit-O-Honeys, Smarties, and Tootsie Rolls to the outstretched hands of these starving youngsters.

Ron had joined our unit two months ago and from the start you could tell that this well-built but pudgy farm boy from Arkansas had a heart of gold. He was a timid, shy kind of guy, which seemed unusual for a boy who had five brothers and two sisters, but he definitely had a way with people that set him apart from the reality of the situation. It didn't matter that he was stuck here in this war-ridden country with his life at stake every minute of the day, there were people around him that needed his caring ways. Kids who never knew a close family unit like he had on his Arkansas farm. Kids who had spend the better part of their lives begging for food from the strangers.

It didn't take anyone in our unit long to learn Ron's good natured characteristics and it was hard for anyone not to really like the guy.

The average age of our unit was about nineteen years old, so Ron was one of the few that were married. His wife was, of course, his high school sweetheart and they had their first baby three months before Ron was shipped to Nam. He was naturally as close to his new family as his old, and cherished the daily letter that arrived at mail call. We'd often kid him about having a family the size of his parents by saying that he could never re-enlist to stay in the service because he wouldn't have time to "build his baseball team."

> *Sometimes I really feel like getting a place of my own! There, I've said it! I've always thought about it but never said it. I've always lived at home and most of the time really enjoy being around my family and Doretta. But occasionally I just get the urge to grow up and become independent–get an apartment and live life to the fullest (Ha-Ha! This is not the real Patty talking here!). Sometimes I wonder if living at home is stunning my emotional growth, but then I always seem to bounce back to reality and realize that I'd probably go stark-raving mad. Just imagine trying to amuse yourself mentally every night, that's not for me. I couldn't stand being alone! Don't you ever feel that way? Of course you do, look where you are (stupid girl!) – but that's not really true. You're not alone because I'm always with you...*

We finally made our way to the main highway, which at least was somewhat of a harder surface and two vehicles wide. This was the most dangerous part of our trip though, because we were in the open with just wall-to-wall rice paddies on both sides for miles upon miles. We were on our best guard for something to happen, but the biggest job was Mo's who as lead vehicle had to keep an especially keen eye on the road for fear of land mines.

Land mines were the gooks way of letting us know they knew we used these roads frequently. Most of the time they were too unequipped to hit us even if they had us within sight, but a strategically placed land mine in the road did enough damage to the vehicles and troops.

In the distance we could hear and see explosions apparently from arty or aircraft; a sight and sound that became a normal commonplace occurrence over here. Ron used to say the sounds almost made him feel at home because it reminded him of the ever present summer storms that would constantly rumble over the fields, filling the Arkansas sky with clouds of thunder.

It took us about four hours to reach DaNang airfield and we immediately headed for the eastern sector of the field that housed the supply depot for incoming goods. To our surprise, DaNang had been hit the night before so everything seemed to be a little more hectic and disruptive than usual.

As we pulled off to the side of the tall oblong building, Joe jumped off the back and Diff and I climbed out with our beer requisition in hand. Ron was the last to jump out of the back but immediately headed in the direction of a small Vietnamese girl who looked to be about five years old and was venturing towards the main thoroughfare of the busy airfield.

"Hey sweetheart, where do you think you're goin', we have a date to go shopping in the PX over here?" Ron said as he swept the little girl up to his shoulders. He was tickling her and bobbing up and down as he jerkily ran across the road towards the airfield post-exchange. I could here him muttering wildly in a kiddie voice to her as if he had known her for years and was placed their solely for the purpose of babysitting her for the afternoon.

After about a half an hour of paperwork, and fifteen people later, we finally were told where to get our cargo and I grabbed the keys from Diff to move the truck to the side entrance of the depot building. It was only a matter of minutes before the supply depot crew had loaded the six hundred fifty cases of beer on our truck and it was definitely a sight to behold. The back of the truck was packed solid, top to bottom, side to side, with cases of beer. Unbelievable! I had never seen so much beer in one place in my entire life.

The three of us piled into the front of the truck and drove over to the PX to pick up Ron for the journey back to Phu Bai as Mo followed in the jeep. Just as we stopped the truck and were piling out, the front screen door opened and out walked Ron with the little girl still in his arms. Her smiling face was now shadowed by a huge red bow that was set on top of her head with little polka dot streamers flowing down the front. One jaw was puffed out so big you would have thought a golf ball was in her mouth instead of five pieces of candy. One hand held a fistful of black licorice, while the other strangled a bottle of Coke that was half empty. Ron immediately saw we were ready to roll and knew we wanted to be back to base well before sundown. He bounced her off his waist and glided her gently to the ground as he slowly knelt on one knee beside her.

"Well sweetheart," he said in his best Humphrey Bogart voice, "it's time for you and I to say good-bye."

The two of them hesitated for what seemed like ten minutes as they stared eye to eye. Her big brown eyes were intense with a river of emotion as her long eyelashes brushed aside the wave of tears.

"Here's lookin' at you kid." His clenched fist grazed her jaw as he muttered the famous line. She had already started to leap, open-armed, around his neck.

The hug and good-bye could have lasted a day but being the kind of guy Ron is he would not let it end this way.

"Look what's behind that little cute ear of yours," he said. "A big beautiful Arkansas red rose." As quick as a magician displays a rabbit, Ron pulled a large silk rose from behind her head and held it out for her to take.

"Take this, Kathy, and always remember GI Joe, okay?"

He quickly turned and jumped on the rear bumper of the truck and I was right behind him. Diff climbed into the cab as Joe jumped into the jeep to ride shot-gun with Mo as we were off on our homeward journey, hopefully incident free.

Ron and I stretched out on top of the cases of beer, our heads on our hands, staring at the sky above.

"How in the world did that little girl get an American name like

Kathy?" I said as I glanced over at Ron.

"Oh, she didn't...Kathy is my little girl's name." A tear rolled down his cheek as he stared straight up at the blue sky puffed with billowy white clouds. Clouds that we both wished were American clouds.

We headed north as fast as we could, not quite as cautiously as we should have been, but nevertheless in a hurry to get to Phu Bai and engulf our mind, body, and soul in this delicious cargo we were delivering.

The majority of the trip was spent sunbathing—I'll never as long as I live forget sunbathing on top of six hundred fifty cases of beer in South Vietnam—laying back just thinking of places I'd rather be.

> *I went down to the beach today and just laid back and soaked up the rays. The day was beautiful and I couldn't think of anyplace I'd rather be, except you weren't there! I spent a lot of time daydreaming (a usual pastime for me – especially at work) and most of the time it was of you. When I opened my eyes you weren't beside me. Oh well, maybe someday, huh? I wish you were here now so we could talk...*

As our small two-vehicle convoy headed north up Route 1, the highway was again a bustle of activity, loaded with civilian buses and motor scooters. We passed a small six-vehicle convoy of ARVN (Army of the Republic of Vietnam) soldiers heading south towards DaNang loaded with supplies, weapons, and even some cases of beer. We hit a small straightaway lined with rice paddies on both sides, each paddy green with life, dikes around each one, holding ankle deep water. The entire area was a patchwork of grids as the individual farms of rice were divided and sectioned to hold its harvest. The road narrowed slightly ahead as the open fields of rice paddies gave way to a forest of trees and open field on the right side and the hills of a small range of mountains beginning on the left.

As we moved around the bend in the road and started up a small incline we were startled by the pop of rifle fire from inside the tree line to our right. In a matter of milliseconds, Ron and I had grabbed our rifles lying beside us and were poised in a prone position on top of our cargo. As our two vehicles slowed down from the incline of the hill, we began to pull to the opposite side of the road against the hills. As the occasional popping of a few guns could be heard, we focused our attention towards the trees as our jeep and truck pulled over to the side of the road with the hills to our back. I couldn't understand why we were stopping instead of giving it everything we had to get up the hill and the hell out of there— although Ron and I were sitting targets on top of these cases of beer.

"What the hell we stopping for?" I yelled as Ron and I slithered off the side of the truck. "We could get pinned down here real easy."

"I was afraid to zip up the road," answered Mo as he and Joe ran over beside the truck with Diff and I. "If these gooks planned this ambush, they could have planted a few mines up the road figuring we'd make a quick break for it. I thought maybe our chances would be better here."

"Yeah, I guess you're right," said Ron.

The shots were beginning to ring out at a faster pace now that we had stopped, as we realized that we were in fact the designated target. The ricochet of two rounds hit the side of the hill behind us as a brief cloud of dust rose into the air.

"Those damn gooks are shootin' at us!" said Joe as we all glanced at the hillside hits.

"I tell you one thing, if they hit any of our beer they're gonna wish they had never got up this morning," yelled Diff as he glanced over the fender of the truck towards the tree line.

"Ya know, I can see the damn muzzle flashes up in the treetops over there. Looks like four or five of them. Why don't we open up on them before they do some real damage. Mo, why don't you make your way over to the jeep once we open fire and get on the radio. See if you can get Ladybug." Diff pointed towards the jungle brush on the other side of the road as he planned our retaliation.

"Okay, let's do it," Joe said as he positioned himself by the front tire of the truck.

"I'll take the rear of the truck," I yelled, running to the back tire and falling down on one knee. I unbuckled my cartridge belt and laid the fully loaded clips beside my foot, ready to reload when ready.

Ron ran to the front side of the jeep while Mo edged his way to the open side of the jeep ready to grab the radio as soon as we opened fire.

The firing was continuing at a steady rate now as we could hear rounds bouncing off the hood and sides of the truck and jeep.

"Okay, let's getum before they get lucky and hit one of our gas tanks or something. Do it!" shouted Diff as he opened up fire at the tree line enemies.

We all let loose and began peppering the trees with M-16 fire from four different angles. The shots being returned almost stopped as we could see what looked like movement and rustling from the tops of the trees. Mo could be heard above the gunfire trying desperately to reach Ladybug, but as we feared the hills we were using to protect our back side was blocking any hope of sending or receiving a radio signal.

A body dropped from one treetop as we drenched the leaves with what seemed like hundreds of rounds. As we slowed our fire we could hear only an occasional rifle pop in return of our fire.

As I stopped firing and reached for another clip of ammo, I could see the outlined figures of men jumping down out of the trees and spreading out along the wood line perpendicular to the road. They seemed to be forming a line and, as fast as I observed their formation, they began to charge out from the trees running across the field towards the road.

"They're charging us, guys. Let's getum'!" I yelled as I forced the clip into my rifle and raised it to my shoulder, taking aim at the figure charging us on the far right side. He was running at a quickening pace as he fired his rifle wildly from side to side, not even bothering to take aim. I watched him through my rifle sights as the entire sequence seemed to move in slow motion. A make-shift hat was flopping on top of his head held down by a scarf tied around his chin. He had on black colored semi-camouflaged trousers and his dirt-colored shirt was flapping behind him, showing his bare young chest. He was yelling and screaming, as they all were, as they ran their suicide course across the low thick open field.

I jolted myself back to reality, trying to remember that the closer he got the more chance one of his rounds would hit me directly or ricochet into someone else. I slowly aimed directly at his mid-section and gently squeezed the trigger, holding it for a short quick burst. By the time I hit him he was about twenty feet from the road and his rifle, a Russian carbine, flew into the air as he grabbed his chest and hit the ground like a brick. I quickly moved my rifle over to find another target only to see the other four charging soldiers falling to the ground also. I moved my sights back over to my man to see if there was any movement from his small-framed body. There was none. His carbine had flown off to his side and was sticking straight up in the air, stuck in the ground by the spiked bayonet attached to the rifle barrel. As I cautiously pulled the rifle away from my eye I glanced back and forth across the field seeing no movement except the waving grass of the field that swept gently with the breeze.

We slowly got up off our knees without looking at each other, not wanting to take our eyes off the field for fear we may turn away prematurely.

The silence was broken by Mo who had watched the action from beside the radio jeep, as he stood holding a grenade in case they got too close.

"Damn crazy gooks. Why'd they do that?"

"Cause it's the only way they know how to do things," said Diff, as he finally turned his attention away from the field and back to us.

"Let's go over and make sure they're dead," said Joe as he reloaded his rifle with a fresh clip of ammo.

"Okay," said Ron, "we gotta get their ammo and weapons anyway so no civilian kids will wander over and get it."

"Go ahead," motioned Diff, "you three check'um out, but be careful. Make sure they're not laying there with a grenade ready for one of you guys."

Ron, Joe, and I lifted our rifles back up and spread apart as we walked around the truck crossing to the far side of the road.

"Hey, Mo," I yelled as I glanced back at the jeep, "keep the wood line covered in case something happens."

"Okay, G, you got it." Mo grabbed Diff's rifle and stood between the truck and jeep with one foot propped on its bumper.

We made our way through the brush as a dense fog seemed to suddenly sift into the area and begin rising from the open field. The sun was beginning to dip behind the hills as its rays danced off the low lying fog. As we walked in our spread out column, I kept focusing to where the gook I shot had dropped, yet my eyes continually darted up to the tree line as I wondered if more of them were watching us, just waiting to make their move. Everything was still as I moved closer heading directly for the swaying rifle that was stuck in the mud, barrel first. The body now came into sight as I stopped cautiously and aimed my rifle directly at the motionless body just in front of me. Both of his arms were raised over his head in front of him, so I knew he didn't have a grenade or knife just waiting for me to get close enough. As I approached him he lie still, unmoving, apparently without a trace of life. As I stood beside him I lightly kicked with my foot waiting for what I hoped would be no reaction. He was still.

I pushed him over and saw the front of him, blood-soaked and riddled with holes from his chest to his groin. It seemed as if every shot found its mark. I reached down and undid his ammo belt and walked over to retrieve his rifle. I glanced over at Joe and Ron as they finished the same routine with the other four bodies and were starting to walk towards me with their captured weapons. I headed towards them as I glanced down at the dead soldier, my heart racing and head pounding as I realized I had ended his life.

We converged together and headed back to the road as the sun went fully behind the hill and the fog seemed to thicken. The smell of gunfire was in the air as we silently arrived back at our vehicles with our hands full of goodies.

Diff had surveyed the damage and the vehicles had come out of it okay. We had lost the windshield of the truck and both headlights of the jeep, but worst of all they had hit quite a few cases of beer. Beer was foaming on the road underneath the truck. It was hard to tell how many cases we had lost, but no one was complaining, at least it was beer, not us.

"Well, not much of a price to pay," I said as we threw the AK-47's in the back of the jeep.

"No, I think we did okay. We got boo-coo (many) miles to go so let's head out; we wanna' get the hell out of here before it gets dark." Diff motioned as he climbed up in the truck and we headed back out.

As we pulled away, I glanced back over the lifeless figures lying in the empty field. Here were five men, who fifteen minutes ago were living and now were helpless bundles of flesh, slowly draining the warmness of life. They would not see the sun set tonight, but I would. It bothered me momentarily that I had taken his life—taken him from his family who would grieve when he didn't return. But when I thought of the value of my own life and the situation this war had put me in—his life or mine, I no longer felt bad. I lived, he was dead.

I knew I had killed before, as the lieutenant and I had spotted many large groups of Cong in the fields and called in artillery on them. We watched as they were destroyed like ants, the results of our command. But this was somehow different. This was a confrontation of man against man, one on one. He lost, I won. I liked those results. But nonetheless, today I had killed...

The remainder of our mission ended safely and incident free. Needless to say, the jubilation and wild celebration that greeted our arrival in camp was a sight to behold. The brew would definitely flow tonight, but it would flow for many reasons. It should have been to drown the guilt but it was definitely to celebrate life!

With a human chain formed, we unloaded the precious cargo in an area that resembled a sandbagged tomb. This beer had more protection than most of us had, but it meant more to us than most other things right now. We had no break in the action, no time off without worry, no place to relax without being on full alert, so what time we did have meant a great deal to us. Beer was our escape, our entertainment, our music, and helped us cope with our memories of the past as well as our unpredictable future. We didn't need to get drunk every night to keep our wits, but we needed each other to talk to and something to soothe this inhuman environment.

> *Keep your thoughts on me and Pensacola. I hope you do come here to visit when you get leave. Pensacola is such a fantastic place to visit (and live), there's always something to do and if you run out of ideas, there's always our beautiful beaches. I can't wait to see you and take you there, to the beach, alone...promise you'll come.*

It was really tough on all of us, but guys like Ron who had family at home spent endless hours racking his brain trying to figure out what will become of his wife and kids if something should happen to him. It was our job to keep each other from having these negative thoughts, we had to always think positive or it would be all over.

"Hey, Ron, snap out of it. What ya' thinking about?" yelled Joe as he slapped my arm and pointed to Ron.

"Hey, Ron," I joked. "Better be careful or you'll fall off the edge of the hooch and strangle yourself on your dog tags."

"Yeah, I'm here," Ron answered as he half-smiled while staring into his can of beer. "I was just thinking about Laura and Kathy and what's gonna happen to them if I ..."

"Bullshit—shut-up—I don't want to hear that shit!" yelled Diff. "Nobody here is going home in a body bag, not as long as I'm in charge."

"What's this 'in-charge' crap?" shouted Mike as he popped open another can of Pabst. "I've got 95 days and a wakeup. That makes me the short-timer of the platoon."

"Big shitin' deal!" I shouted. "That and ten P's (Piaster's were Vietnamese money) will buy you a pack of dink cigarettes."

"You'll never go back to The World anyway; you love this place so much you know you'll re-up for more benes (benefits). They'll offer you another stripe and another sixty-five dollars a month combat pay and you'll snap it up faster than a pig in shit," said Sergeant Whitt as he walked to the edge of the hooch and jumped down to sit with us.

"You tell'um, Sarge!"

"You gotta be shittin' me, ain't no goddamn way I'm stayin' in this filthy slant-eye country. Uncle Sam ain't got enough shitin' money in his budget to get me to swing another tour over here. So stick that in your can of beer, Sarge."

"Okay, Mike I got your message," laughed Sergeant Whitt as he popped open a can of beer. "So, how's the mail treating you guys? You still feeding all those lines of bullshit to your love back home, Joe?"

"Yeah, Linda and I are doing okay. She'll wait, she knows a good thing when she's got it!"

"How about you, G, heard from Patty lately?"

"You bet," I said as I lit a cigarette. "It's a good thing I got her, cause I'd be lost if I counted on the rest of my women to write regular."

Just as the talk was getting good our arty started shelling positions to our west that we had plotted that day. It was almost useless to try and talk over the guns, so we finished our drinks and turned in for the night. It didn't take me long to put this Pabst Blue Ribbon day behind me and start thinking about home and Patty. After incidents like today, I wondered if I'd ever see her at all.

> *I've been going out occasionally, but none of the guys seem to interest me. I think I'm comparing them to you too much. I mean we talk so easily and have so much in common as far as our likes and dislikes, and they're all a bunch of jerks (now,now Patty, don't be too hard on them). I guess I shouldn't compare everyone to you but I just can't help it – you're for me and that's that. Be extra careful, Gar..."*

MY SOUTHERN BELLE

I tossed and turned most of the night trying to forget what had happened on the road that day and trying to forget the faces of the young kids in black pajamas we had cut down in the field. I usually didn't have a problem getting to sleep, but the incidents of the day kept creeping into my mind. Every time I would finally drift off I'd wake up to a rat snuggling in beside me trying to keep warm. The rats were one of our biggest problems—there were just so damn many of them, we couldn't control or manage them. They were so common because of the rice paddies where they lived and bred. We'd usually spray our hooches about every two weeks with pesticide, but within a day or two they'd be right back with us. I can remember finishing up FDC (Fire Direction Control) watch late at night and coming back to my hooch to get some sleep. I'd walk in the door and shine the flashlight down the row of cots and laying with each guy was one or two rats just cuddling up to stay warm. Most guys would sleep with their poncho covers all tucked up in their air mattresses so the rats couldn't get close to them. But you could always feel them beside you when you rolled over. I never remember seeing too many of them during the daylight hours but at night it was a different story. I'm really surprised no one got bit more often but that just didn't seem to be a problem. I guess the rats really didn't have any place to live underground, since the gooks had tunneled up the whole damn country, so they decided just to keep us company!

I was really put through the paces at work today
and came home simply exhausted; I didn't even want

to see food (which is highly unusual for me). All the way home I thought how great it's going to be to just take a bath, do my hair, and crawl in bed. Then I found your letter. Your letters are like medicine to me – a hypnotic trance that cures all evil and rids the body of any pain and discomfort (sounds like Love Potion #9). Anyway I did skip dinner but I did take you to the bathtub with me, my favorite spot with my favorite guy. Your letters are so great because I get so much out of what you say. I have to read them several times and each time I read more meaning in between the lines. I'm now laying in bed writing to you – I wish you were here (and so do you probably)... (now, now Patty!). Well, I won't go into details but...I hope you sleep well tonight...

As the next day dawned, we seemed to celebrate life even more than before. I think we all realized how serious the ambush on the road could have turned out, we were definitely an easy target for any gook patrol.

As we left the mess hall from a normal appalling meal, we were greeted by mail call much earlier today than it usually is. We usually got mail every day, sometimes every other day, but the sight of that bright red mail sack being thrown off a chopper was something that brought a ray of sunshine even on the gloomiest days; and gloomy days were commonplace over here. I don't believe you ever really get used to war, but it does become somewhat routine just like everything else in life. The whole attitude over here is a little like the television show *M*A*S*H*, I mean here was a group of guys in a war, thousands of miles from home and they let their humor and pranks run their lives in the 4077th MASH Unit. You absolutely have to do that! You have to forget the bad things when they're not happening and have some fun, enjoy your buddies. It didn't matter if we played cards, drank beer, sang songs, or told jokes—we needed that release valve, that good time to savor life and add a little meaning to our day to day existence.

Well, today I finally did it – I went to the store and bought a bathing suit. This one is not the usual classic and conservative Patty – this is the unknown Patty. It's extremely feminine and looks grrrrreat on me, but I'm scared to wear it. Now that I've bought it, what will I do with it? I just can't imagine me having the nerve to wear it to the beach (oh go ahead, Patty; the guys will fall at your feet). It looks great on me and I'll do it!!

………I went to the beach today and wore my same old bathing suit!

Mail call was one of our fun times too. It was one of the few times you were glad to hear your name called out. As usual with everything in the service you waited and waited for your turn to come. Joe hadn't received a letter in two days so as his name was called a smile came over both our faces, especially when he got three letters.

"Hey, Joe, leave some mail for the rest of us!" I joked as he ran each letter under his nose trying to pick up a good scent.

"Without even looking, I can tell this one's from Linda. Oooohhhh, some real nice smell—she outdid herself this time. Gimme a smoke, G, I'll meet ya in the hooch, okay?"

"Sure, pal, make us a drink. I'll be right there," I said as I threw him a cigarette.

He took off for our hooch, half running, still sniffing the letter from Linda.

"Good luck!" he yelled without even turning around.

As I heard the call of my initial, I was surprised as I saw what was coming at me—not a letter but a large envelope.

As I walked back to my hooch, I really can't describe the anticipation that ran throughout my body. It was a moment I had thought about for so long, yet it was almost scary for it to finally arrive; would I be disappointed? Would it change how I felt about her? Is appearance that important to me? I mean, here is a girl who I have intimately known "verbally" for seven months now and I am totally in love with her personality, her characteristics, her style, her verbal expression, her...but now, what does finally seeing her face do to me? I've seen her face in words many times throughout our relationship but even that still leaves some imaginary flexibility on my part.

Hundreds of thoughts raced frantically through my mind as I tightly gripped the brownish-yellow 8x10 envelope; wanting to rip it open and savor the face of my dream girl, but shunning the thought of having anything spoil the beautiful image I have built of her.

It was getting dark and I knew most of the guys in our hooch would either be on watch duty or over at the beer hooch drowning the day's sorrows; but I could see a small dim light as I approached the door so I knew Joe was there. He was sitting on the edge of his cot just folding back a letter he had read and I could tell by the lonely homesick look on his Italian face that he wasn't in the mood for being in Vietnam at that moment.

"How's Linda doing?" I asked as I threw my mail on the cot.

"Great, G, just great except for the fact that she's there and I'm here! I don't know why I look forward to mail call so much. Its supposed t be a morale booster, but shit man, it's depressing as hell. How am I supposed to remain sane when my goddamn beautiful luscious girl is home, fourteen thousand damn miles away from me writing me letters saying she misses the hell out of me! How, G, tell me how?"

"Well, you know what they say; it gives you something to fight for."

"Sure, man, but we got four shittin' months of this crap left...I'll never make it!"

"Hey, the hell you won't. We're gonna beat this thing, Joe. You and me and Diff—we're gonna get out of this godforsaken country and out of this pussy-ass Marine Corp and party, party, party. We're gonna make the Mardi Gras look like a kid's birthday party compared to the celebratin' we're gonna do!"

"Yeah, I sure as hell hope so, man. I keep thinking about how one of us could be next....it's such a waste."

"Hey, cut the bullshit, we're gonna make it—now gimme a smoke and break out my bottle of Southern Comfort, we're gonna have a drink to celebrate."

"Celebrate? Celebrate what?" asked Joe as he popped open my foot locker and hoisted out my latest bottle of 100 proof Southern Comfort whiskey.

"See what's laying on that cot?" I said as I lit the cigarette he threw to me.

"Holy shit, did you get a picture from Patty?"

"Yep, do you believe it—she finally came through after all this time."

"Well, if we're celebratin' she must be nice...let me see, damn it!"

I glanced over at Joe with that shit-eatin' smile on his face and could just read the surprise and anticipation written all over his face.

"No," I said. "I haven't looked yet."

"Well, what the hell you waitin' for, mail call was fifteen minutes ago. Are you crazy? As long as you have been waitin' for a flick from this chick and you haven't looked yet?"

"I can't, Joe...I just can't. I gotta have a drink first."

"Aw, come on, man, you can't be worried. Nobody could write letters the way she does and be a dog. She's gonna be gorgeous."

"Sure, Joe. I guess if you were in my shoes you would have looked by now, right...just rip open the envelope and look, right? ... Well?"

"Okay... let's drink!" Joe laughed as he handed me a martini glass and opened the bottle. He knew damn well that sometimes it took him two days to open a letter if he knew there was something out of the ordinary about the contents.

We both poured a drink and sat down on our lawn chairs beside our cots. We were so much alike in our ways that it almost seemed as if we were brothers by blood, yet this war had taken two strangers and brought us so close together that we needed each other like family. We could depend on each other during our highs and lows; our traumas and celebrations; our good times and bad.

"Did she write a letter too?" asked Joe as he picked up the brown envelope to examine it.

"No, not unless there's one inside. I guess I'm kinda' glad too…I'm not sure I could handle a letter and picture in the same day. And knowin' her, she probably realized that fact!"

Joe sunk deep down in his chair as he fondled the envelope and nearly spilled his drink in his lap.

"I can't believe this chick, G," said Joe as he threw me the envelope. "Take a whiff of the perfume smell this has after traveling fourteen thousand miles!"

I just about went ape-shit as I sniffed the envelope. You gotta be shittin' me—nobody could get to me the way this girl has. She's just not real! I just can't look—I just can't open this and ruin what we have together.

"Who said you're gonna ruin it…she's gotta be as gorgeous as her letters…how many ugly southern belles have you seen in your day…none…not one! You just listen to ol' Joe and open that goddamn envelope, my Italian intuition has never failed us yet!"

"Well, one more drink and I think I'll be ready." I reached for the bottle and filled both of our glasses to the brim.

"Did you know she finally sent a flick or was it a total surprise?"

"Well, one letter about two weeks ago she said she was going to a photographer and have a descent picture taken, but knowing how she hates pictures of herself I kind of shrugged it off as just another line to pacify me for a while. But now—damn it, here it is!"

I stared at the envelope in my hand almost as if I were in a trance. The handwriting was as her handwriting always is, neat, feminine, and almost perfect. So often I had been criticized about my handwriting, that it was so neat and stylish like a draftsman; but hers was written as beautifully as the words it formed.

"Would you rather be alone while you open it?" asked Joe in a small understanding yet sincere voice.

"No," I said. "I came back to the hooch to be alone and ponder my fate, but I'd much rather we take this hurdle together. I mean if this girl is a dog you're the one who's gonna suffer with me!"

I turned the glass ‘bottoms up’ as I chugged the last of my drink and handed the empty glass to Joe to fill up again. I grabbed the envelope, gently forced open the taped flap, and settled back in my chair to savor the moment…the moment of truth!

I slowly opened the flap and began inching the picture up out of the envelope until it was fully exposed. Here was an 8x10 black and white glossy of the girl I had intimately known for seven months now, and who was as much a part of my life as my family.

Her hair was medium short and styled perfectly around her bright smiling face. She had small facial features dominated by smallish eyes and a smile that would melt an ice cube. The signature across the lower right-hand corner read

Yours ‘til Birnum Wood comes to Dunsinane, Patty!

Perfect…that was her style. Not just “Love Always” or “Yours Forever,” but a Shakespearian quote that said it in a way only she knew how. She was beautiful!

I looked up at Joe and he leaped from his chair, shoveled down his drink and smashed the empty glass down on the floor into a million pieces.

“I knew it, I knew it! I can tell by that shit-eatin’ smile on your face that she’s gorgeous. Let me see, damn it—share the wealth with your ol’ New York buddy.”

I handed the flick to Joe and the expression on his face was over shadowed only by the glow on mine.

“Holy shit, G. She’s fantastic, man, a livin’ doll! Have you ever seen a gorgeous mystifying smile like that before? …hey, G…hello, hello, are you there?”

I was in another world; a world that had me fourteen thousand miles away on a little deserted beach in Pensacola, Florida, next to a girl that was staring into my eyes, talking with her smile, and caressing me with her eyes. My dream was now complete. The girl that I had talked to for so long had finally answered me in a way that expressed her deepest feelings. The words were written on the picture but expressed so beautifully in her eyes and smile. Her hair was perfect for her face, medium length, brunette, with her bangs sweeping gently across her forehead to one side. Her small eyes and nose accented her lips just giving her that southern look. For now she was mine, and for this one short moment in time we were together only for each other.

"Hello, Corporal Lusby, hello!" groaned Joe as he shook my shoulder. "Earth to Gary, Earth to Gary!"

"Yeah, I'm back," I moaned as I recovered from my fantasy trip to Patty's side. "I really need a drink now, Joe…freshen this one up for me, okay?"

"You got it, pal. Hey, that fantasy has got to come true. I know as sure as I'm standin' here that your ass will be in Florida as soon as we get back to The World and out of this godforsaken Marine Corp. You two will meet and just set Pensacola on fire…Yowl!!!!"

"Okay, mad dog, settle down," I said as I grabbed Joe by the shirt pulling him down off of his cot. "Let's not get too carried away—we gotta make it out of this hell-hole first."

"C'mon, G, that's a piece-a-cake for you and me. First of all, we're too damn tough and ornery for anybody to waste their time trying to blow us away. Second of all, who the hell is gonna drink all the booze that the US Government keeps sending over here. Third, nobody in their right mind would even think of depriving all those gorgeous blue-eyed women back home the privilege of our company…men of the world that we are! And fourth, we…"

"Okay, okay! I'm convinced. But you better just make damn sure that you notify everyone over here, so they know to lay off!"

"Have no fear, have no fear. The New York Italian has spoken!" Joe recited as he stepped up on top of his cot raising his right hand and saluting with his drink.

I heard what Joe was saying, I just wish it was all that easy. There were just so many obstacles in your way it was hard to imagine anyone getting out of here alive. The damn gooks fought their crazy war at night when nobody could see what the hell was going on, instead of the daytime when every other war was fought. There were many things you got used to or immune to as the war went on, but few men got over the fear of moving through the jungle at night, in the unseen presence of an enemy who was at home in the darkness. When you moved in the darkness, you wanted your friends close to you, in sight, and when a firefight erupted you frantically fired wildly at the enemy hoping to waste every gook within range. When you did go out in the field, you had to fight every step of the way so you didn't get blown apart by a land mine, or walk into a Malayan Gate that would whip into you burying poison spikes into your body. If you survived the gooks you had to worry whether the artillery rounds and B-52 bombs you called for were going to wipe out the enemy or fall on top of you by mistake. If all that wasn't bad enough, just last week some asshole staff sergeant in another unit got his ass fragged out in the field by his own men, or at least that's the word we got. So now if the gooks didn't get you, and the bombs didn't get you, then some jerk-off in the next hooch who didn't like you will. With all of this bullshit, it's hard for us to believe that people wonder why we drink a little beer to quell our nerves. What a small price to pay for something good in this miserable environment!

I couldn't take my eyes off of her picture. This was the first time I had gazed upon her beautiful eyes, but it was special. I felt as if I knew her and her me. I finally saw my southern belle.

THE SOUNDS OF DEATH

Joe had stepped down off of his pedestal and was making a new batch of drinks. I almost sensed his abrupt quietness as he let me savor the moment of Patty and I getting acquainted. The quietness of the still night was interrupted only by the glass stirrer clinking against the side of the pitcher as a fresh batch of scotch and water's were born and ready for consumption.

The night was unusually quiet. It was starting to get darker much earlier in the evening now, but the hustle and bustle of pedestrian traffic around the camp just didn't seem as noticeable today as it usually does. I looked at Joe as if something seemed to click.

"I thought you were getting a haircut today?" I asked.

"Yeah, I was going to, but the gooks never showed up today, the tent was wrapped up tight."

I jumped up and glanced at the row of tents that lined our eastern perimeter. It was empty, no activity, no signs of life.

"Oh shit," I said. "Joe, I bet we're getting hit tonight."

"What the hell are you talking about, G? I think Patty's flick has you in a trance."

"No man, I'm not kiddin'! The gooks didn't show up today, none of them. When's the last time you can remember all the gooks takin' off on the same day? In fact, when's the last time you remember the gooks takin' off at all and passing up more of our hard-earned bucks? That means something's going on! C'mon we gotta' tell, Sarge!"

I tore out of the hooch trying to button my shirt as I ran. Joe was right behind me yelling he would head for Sergeant Whitt's hooch while I headed for Sergeant Danson's.

There wasn't much activity in the whole camp; just about everyone was either at the 'watering hole' grabbing a beer, or in the mess hall eating dinner.

I ran past the mess hall and down through the sandbagged walls into Sergeant Danson's hooch.

"Sarge, you in here?" I yelled as I glanced around the empty hooch. I could see his flak jacket and rifle laying on the bunk, so I knew he wasn't making his rounds.

Whipping back out of the sarge's tent, I turned quickly and knocked over half a wall of sand bags. I figured he must be in the club hooch since his favorite time of the day was tipping a few beers at the end of the evening. I headed back to the club hooch and as I looked up I could see Joe running back towards me from the club. As I grabbed the door to the club hooch and stepped in, my fear became reality.

A volley of explosions could be heard at the southern end of camp. I froze in my tracks as the door to the hooch swung into my back. I was stunned as I turned back only to have the door pulled back open by Joe as he pushed me aside screaming frantically.

"Incoming, Incoming!" he cried as the echo of those two words rang throughout the camp.

The hooch was now a frenzy of activity as everyone jumped to their feet knocking over tables, chairs, and trays.

The thumping of the 82mm mortar fire was continuing in the distance but seemed to be walking closer as each trio of explosions stepped towards us. Our camp was about one-half square mile in area, with bunkers, trenches, and outposts encircling us. Artillery guns were positioned on all four sides with the largest and strongest contingent to our west and north. Unlike other wars where we captured ground and held our own, Vietnam was a jungle of villages, mazes, tunnels, and dense terrain. The only way we could capture ground and keep it was to position our artillery and forces there, and hold it. Once we turned the ground over to the 'friendlies,' it was just a matter of time before the gooks tunneled themselves and their supplies back in and took it over. The westerly direction from our camp showed the most jungle and enemy infiltration routes, while the northern guns were primarily to give protection to the town of Hue. Hue was the largest city in our area with an immense cultural history. It was at one time the Imperial City to Vietnam. We were separated from Hue by the Perfume River, which was on the southern side of the city. Directly to the west of Hue was the A Shau Valley coming down from Khe Sanh and running along the eastern border of Laos, which was the strategic location right in the line of major supply routes to and from the DMZ.

"Everyone hit the bunkers and work your way to the perimeter," shouted Sgt. Danson. "Remember the attack drills!"

Our attack drill was like a choreographed ballet with each cast member learning his part of the script. Each member had his routes, his assigned duties, and his responsibilities; all contributing to the 'team effort.' The many practices that we had every day had led each of us to react instinctively without taking valuable time to think or make decisions. Our only variable was getting from where we stood now, to our assigned route. After that we were robots enacting a scene.

Joe and I turned back out of the door and pulled each other along as we ran towards the sand-bagged bunker outside the club hooch. Before the screen door could halfway close, Diff came barreling out, knocking the door off of its top hinge and into the front wall of the hooch. With one gigantic leap we were all in the bunker with the echoing of explosions beginning to walk through our immediate area. We sat unusually quiet and let our experience of the situation control our reactions and emotions. Diff had immediately started timing the volleys and was alertly pulling more guys into our already packed bunker as the incoming continued.

"Three rounds every thirty seconds," he snapped as everyone listened intently trying to pinpoint exactly what location the volley of rounds were striking now. "We'll wait two more volleys, if they continue every thirty seconds we'll make our break to the next bunker."

"Has anyone figured out the impact area yet?" a voice asked from the rear of the bunker.

"Sounds to me like their hittin' in the middle of the goddamn compound," said Jenkins, a new recruit to our outfit. "I'll be damned if I'm moving from this spot until that fuckin' shellin' stops! I'm not gettin' my ass plastered all over the area. Maybe you guys want to ma..."

"Shut-up!" snapped Diff. "Shut-up and follow the damn routine you've been taught or your young ass will be dog meat anyway!"

Jenkins was shaking like crazy as his eyes widened. He had joined our outfit about ten days ago from the states and it was obvious this was his first taste of action. Joe put his arm around Jenkins and calmed him down as Diff looked around at the rest of us to see who was crammed in this tiny hell-hole with him. Diff had always been a people-type person. Someone that everyone either likes immediately or hates, but gains an immense amount of respect and admiration for. He always seemed to be a born leader, which is one reason his sergeant stripe couldn't be too far off.

"Okay, Diff, we got a new guy here, I'll take him," said Joe as he motioned for Diff to lay off. As I watched Joe calmly whisper to Jenkins at the rear of the bunker, I could tell that he knew Jenkins had been on the verge of breaking. Joe, after being over here in Nam for eight months, knew the situation had to be handled in the right way, and immediately.

"Okay...after the next volley we gotta' go. Remember, the first order of business is to get to your hooches and get your gear, then head for your assigned areas. Anybody got a problem?" asked Diff.

"Yeah, who the hell ordered the fireworks, we don't need this shit tonight?" snapped Tony from the back corner.

"I don't know," said Diff, "but this is no time to take pictures. Jenkins, why don't you be Joe's shadow. Joe, where you headed?"

"I grab a radio, head straight for perimeter south and watch for frontal movement, if I see anything I call arty for some light."

"Great, sounds good, you two head for the hooch, grab your shit, and high-tail right down to the line. Jenkins, don't you dare leave Joe's side, got it?"

"We got it…right, pal, stick with me, no sweat!" Joe assured him as he slapped the brim of Jenkins cap.

What Jenkins was going through jogged the memories of all of us. The first realization that you're in a combat zone is the most terrifying moment in your young military life. It really doesn't matter that you've been through months of training just to prepare for this moment. It doesn't matter what your background is or what your age or time-in is…this is your life that's at stake and the reality of where you are and what's happening is devastating. Hell, this is our fourth shelling in a month and I'm sure no one ever gets "used" to it.

I'll never forget those first nights in Dong Ha that I spent scared out of my wits. Laying in my bunk each night trying to decipher outgoing artillery from incoming mortars. I was so elated when I found out that I would be part of an artillery unit, feeling that I would have all the protection I needed from those big guns. It was reassuring to know what I had on my side, but each night the "boom" of the howitzers echoing through the stillness of the night air would bring me erect in my bunk wondering if this was it! It really takes many, many nights of conditioning the mind to separate the sounds of a Vietnamese night; especially as part of an artillery unit where many hours of the night are spent expending rounds of shells into the enemy areas.

Suddenly, the silence was broken by the sounds of explosions closer yet than before. The stillness within the bunker was interrupted only by the conscientious continuous counting by each of us as each of the three explosions met the earth. As the second round hit, Diff yelled.

"Get ready, schools out on the next bell!"

Everyone was quickly shuffling and jockeying for position realizing we would have about thirty seconds to exit and begin our relay.

Ba-Boom!

"Go!"

Off we went as our single-file centipede of soldiers each took off, each destined to break his own land-speed record.

Diff, Joe, Jenkins, and I were all headed for the same hooch. As we hit the front door and ran for our cots the whistling of our immediate enemy, incoming rounds, could be heard as it cut through the still night air.

"Hurry up, here they come!" shouted Joe as we each threw on our helmets and flak jackets.

"Hurry," cried Jenkins. "Let's hit the bunker out front."

"No time," I yelled. "Hit the deck!"

I barely had my helmet and flak jacket on as I fell to the floor beside my rack hugging the floorboards. The whistling was on top of us as an explosion rocked the area. The peppering of shrapnel hitting the sides of the hooch and coming through the screens showered us with bits and pieces of metal fragments. I slowly reached up over the top of my rack and quickly slipped Patty's picture down to the floor with me. I had waited six months for this flick to come; there was no way I was going to let it get showered with mortar fragments. I gently shoved it between my flak jacket and chest for safe keeping. The explosion seemed to hit just directly to the west of us, close enough to throw shrapnel but still a short distance away.

"Stay down!" Joe yelled as Jenkins began to frantically crawl. Panic was in his eyes as his hands and feet were flapping, uncontrollably.

"I'm not going to die," he cried as tears showed in his eyes. He started to jump up and Joe pounced on him throwing his face to the surface of the floorboards…one of the best body-tackles I've seen in a long time. Joe bear-hugged Jenkins' entire body using his weight to completely disable Jenkins' movements.

The second explosion hit outside our hooch almost directly on the row of hooches across from ours. Shrapnel again peppered the sides of the hooch as pings of metal meeting metal echoed after the explosion.

"Oh shit, we're next!" sobbed Jenkins as the tears on his cheeks sank into the floorboards, his face smashed against the ground under the weight of Joe's body.

"Shut-up and pray," whispered Joe as the silence again began to break with the whistling sound of another incoming round.

As always in situations like this when suddenly you're confronted with a life and death situation, especially when you really have no decisions, you're at the mercy of the environment; your thoughts wander to your life, your loved ones, and what you want to live to return to. It reminded me of a letter Patty had written earlier.

> *In many ways you've become the boy next door, the friend who's always there for me, the pal I never had. It's so great having someone like you to talk to – we've become 'there' for each other, something we both need and look forward to...each other's company. I've grown accustomed to you now – please don't let anything happen to you over there!*

This explosion seemed almost directly in the same area the other was, across from our hooch in the other row; but something was different—something was eerie about this last explosion that seemed to deaden the after silence even more than the last. No shrapnel peppered the hooch, just sounds of after-debris hitting and falling throughout the immediate area and striking the roof.

It was uncanny the way Diff, Joe, and I immediately looked at each other almost sensing the urgency of the situation that we feared was upon us. But we didn't want to verbalize our thoughts, for fear that our comrade Jenkins might panic completely.

Diff broke the silence as he yelled to Joe to get Jenkins into the front bunker before the next volley of rounds was launched. As the two of them grabbed their rifles and ammo clips and ran for the front bunker, Diff and I motioned to each other as we grabbed our gear to head out the rear of the hooch towards the explosion area.

As soon as we were both clear, our inner thoughts were brought to light as we ran towards what used to be Mike and Lenny's hooch. The muffled explosions were cushioned by the direct hit of a mortar round crashing through their roof and exploding inside the environment of our comrades' home.

"Son of a bitch, Diff, we gotta' look for Mike and those guys," I said as I slapped his arm with the back of my hand.

"I know, but stay low and work fast, they'll be coming any second and I got a feelin' we're too damn close for comfort."

"Let's do it!"

We ran through the smoky rumbled mess as if we were walking on hot coals. The entire hooch had been blown to bits with hardly a recognizable piece of gear in sight. It almost seemed too small a pile of rubble to even had been a twelve-man hooch, but it was obvious what a direct hit had done.

There were no signs of movement, only still the occasional falling of debris as if it was being dropped earthward by another being. There was not even a fire, the impact had just blown everything completely apart.

"I don't hear anything. Do you, Diff?"

"No, G, not even a murmur…its too scary to even think about."

"Hopefully no one was in this damn hooch." I said as I shuffled through the aftermath pushing aside things, not really knowing what I was pushing through.

"Okay, let's do it!" Diff shouted, and away we went running in different directions to our assigned areas. I headed for the ammo dump to collect my grenades and rounds, while Diff turned straight for the perimeter to coordinate any frontal action.

We had hardly separated when the whistling of enemy rounds were again interrupting the moment. As I was running I turned and could see Diff zigzagging down past the huge Vietnamese graves that were peppered throughout the compound, waving his fist at them as if to disagree with their meaning of marking death.

I picked up my pace as I felt the concussion of the first round striking the earth with an explosive impact. I stumbled as I was thrown to the ground, still running as if being chased by death itself. The explosion had hit halfway between Mike's hooch, or what was left of it, and where I was now. I could hear the awful sound of the next mortar round as it was released and headed for its destination, which I knew would not be far from where the last round hit. I was still about fifty feet from the nearest bunker so I fell flat on the ground as the second round rocked the area. I lost my helmet as I hit the dirt and rolled with the impact of the explosive force. This one hit just a few yards from the last round. The sounds of the next shell were already in the sky as I frantically put my helmet back on and crawled on all fours away from the area of the last two hits. I didn't want to get up and run for fear the explosive debris would reach me, but as the next round made contact it was obvious my crawling had done no good. The ground ahead of me rumbled as the explosion sent deafening waves of noise throughout the air. A sudden flash of light was brilliant, like that of a flashbulb going off in your eyes, even though I was looking at the ground as I squirmed through the dirt. In an instant I could feel the burning sensation in my arms as if someone had lit tiny matches and tossed them at me. Pellets of metal fragments peppered my helmet and flak jacket, bouncing off as I was flipped over on my back staring at the sky above. I laid motionless as I realized the mortar had exploded in front of me, close enough to send fragments at me, yet far enough away that I was alive and thank god conscious of what was happening. I jumped up and ran for the bunker that was ahead of me knowing that another volley would soon follow and I may not be as lucky when the next round hit. As I bounced in the empty bunker I knew I had made it in plenty of time as I listened for the rounds but heard only the panting of my own breathing and the thumping of my own heartbeat.

I got out my lighter and lit it to look at how bad my wounds were. I could feel the stinging and burning in both my arms but I couldn't feel any pain anywhere else so I figured my arms were the only place hit. The light proved me right as I could see quite a few shrapnel wounds on each arm that were streaming blood with every thump of my heart. It was obvious my helmet and flak jacket had protected my head and body from the force of the shrapnel blast, but my bare groping arms were an open target. It was useless for me to try to clean the wounds, I was sure I would just make things worse, the tiny pieces of hot metal had to come out as soon as possible. The blood was streaming down my arms to my hands making the injury look much worse than it really was—I was thankful to say the least.

It seemed longer than thirty seconds between volleys this time, but again that familiar sound surfaced as explosions again began to rake the area. I shivered involuntarily as I stayed inside the bunker for a few minutes to gather my thoughts, calm down, and most important to make sure the mortars weren't going to get any closer to the ammo dump. I certainly wasn't going near that area if there was the slightest chance of it getting hit. The best thing would be to calm down, catch my breath, and say a prayer. It was times like these you wondered if the next shell had your name on it, if you were the next life to be sacrificed. But you had to forget that and keep your head straight, you had other people depending on you.

> *I love to hear from you, you actually get me through each day at work. I tell the girls at work about you and they seem so jealous. But you're mine, all mine! Stay away, he's mine!! Please keep writing as often as you can, I love to hear from you...and PLEASE be careful...*

After a few minutes I poked my head out of the bunker and could see by the smoke in the distance and the more distant explosions that the mortars were walking their way back to the north side of camp. I grabbed my rifle and headed for the ammo dump zigzagging a pattern across the clearing between hooches, moving just a little faster and crouching just a little lower than I ever had before.

As I arrived at the ammo hooch, Mo was hastily throwing bandoliers of cartridges and grenade boxes out to the ground like he was racing with time. I could see Lt. Barton running from the area having grabbed a box of grenades in each hand as he went by. I threw about a dozen belts over my shoulder and was grabbing another handful when Mo looked out and saw me.

"G, what the hell happened, you okay?"

"Sure, Mo, I'm okay, just caught some shrapnel, nothin' bad." I assured him as I threw more straps over my other shoulder, grabbed some grenades, and off I went.

As I ran towards the perimeter, I was loaded to the hilt. My arms were pounding like crazy as I glanced at the blood covering them in red streaks that glowed brilliant with each flash of light from the sky above; the light coming from our artillery as they lit up the darkness of the night with illumination rounds that seemed to bring the dawn to the middle of the night. The mortar fire had subsided as I ran past the open trenches tossing in straps of ammo, yelling for someone to catch each of my deliveries.

Lt. Barton grabbed me as I ran past the bunker he was in, as he began to question me about my injury.

"Hey, what the hell happened to you?"

"I'm okay," I said. "Just some fragments from a hit that was too close for comfort. I'll get it looked at when we're finished down here."

"Like hell you will," he snapped. "You get your ass up to the medics and get that taken care of now. That could get real serious if its not looked at right away."

"It's not as bad as it looks; I'll go up as soon as ..."

"Now, Corporal Lusby, and that's an order!"

I knew I had met my match. The sternness of his face and the command in his voice was not to be joked with, so off I went. My arms were starting to feel a little numb by now and I figured this was probably the best thing anyway, why take a chance with my own arms.

They dressed up my wounds in no time and it turned out to be less damage than I had thought. I had taken three pieces of shrapnel in my left arm and wrist, and two pieces in my right forearm, all of which came out very easily. Luckily, the explosion was far enough ahead of me that all I caught was a spraying of fragments at the very end of their journey, not the beginning.

I left the medic hooch and was walking back down to the perimeter when I ran into Diff, Joe, and Jenkins running towards me.

"Great night for a stroll in the moonlight, huh?" I yelled as they spotted me.

"There you are," said Joe. "Barton said you got hit going for ammo. You okay, pal?"

"Sure 'nough," I answered as I threw my rifle over my shoulder. "Just got nicked on the surface, nothin' to write home about."

"Hey, how many times we gotta' tell you not to try hand to hand combat with a mortar round, fool," joked Diff as he put both fists up and danced around me, strutting from side to side.

"What can I say, man, gotta keep my reflexes sharp somehow," I said as I slapped the brim of Diff's hat knocking it off in the dirt. "I'd really love to stay here and play with you guys, but I really gotta go now."

"Where the hell you going, you late for a date?" snipped Joe.

"No, I gotta go over to our hooch and change my underwear, I think I shit myself!" I said as I laughed and ran the other way.

They both grabbed me, one on each side, and lifted me up between them, carrying me off like an injured football player being helped to the sidelines. Jenkins, who stood silently, just taking all this in, was shaking his head as if to wonder how much it would take to knock the 'spirit' out of us. Most of us went straight over to the club hooch to reopen it for a few hours and drink our experience away as our arty pounded the mortar sites in answer to their calling.

We were sitting on the steps of the hooch with the doors open talking about the night assault and gazing at the jagged patterns being formed in the sky by the falling illumination rounds, when Sgt. Whitt came up.

"Well, bad news guys, we had one casualty tonight. Brace yourselves because you're not gonna' like this at all. We found Mo down about ten feet from his hooch," he said as his voice quivered with the news.

"Are you shittin' me?" said Diff as he threw his beer down and took off running for Mo's hooch.

"Holy shit, Sarge…can you tell what happened?" I said as a tear rolled down my cheek. "He spent most of the attack at the ammo dump handing out supplies. I just saw him there twenty minutes ago."

"Yeah, it looks like he was heading back to his hooch from the dump when a mortar round hit the hooch. He was probably on his way there to get his helmet and flak jacket and head on down to the perimeter, but since he wasn't wearing it he took a pretty large chunk in the chest. I guess he went from the mess hall straight to the ammo dump when it all started and didn't get his gear first like the rest of us. Damn it, he might have made it if he just had his jacket on!"

We all knew Mo was as dedicated an individual as any one of us here. He never wanted to let anyone get the jump on us, especially the gooks.

"Why don't you two go see how Diff is?" Sgt. Whitt said as he motioned to Joe and I, "you guys know Diff is gonna' take this personally."

Joe and I knew he was right and shook our heads agreeably as we jumped off the steps and headed towards Mo's area. Diff was like a boy scout troop leader when it came to any of us guys; he felt he was accountable for each of us. He would definitely take it hard. As we left, Jenkins began to cry…something we all needed to do.

> *Please take care of yourself over there – tonight I cried thinking of where you really are and what you are doing. You don't tell me much about what's happening to you day to day, but I know that's probably to protect me, not you. I heard someone say a Marine is trained to risk his life for the lives of his buddies in a second…Please be careful!"*

As Joe and I approached our hooch we could see by the darkness that Diff wasn't inside, although we decided to make sure—sometimes the darkness eases the pain and suffering of the hardest times.

"Well, he's not here. Let's head for Mo's area," said Joe, "maybe he's there with Mo."

"You know how pissed off Diff is gonna' be, don't ya?" I said as we shuffled through the red door and headed down the row of hooches.

"Yeah, goddamn Mo came over just a few days after Diff, so they been together the whole shitin' tour. Mo was the only soul-brother we had in our platoon, so he was something special to Diff, like his little black sheep!"

We both chuckled with sadness as we stared at the ground while we walked. It wasn't a time we could joke like we usually did. One of our own was gone. Death was a part of Nam and a part of war, but it was always hardest to face when it hit close to home.

As we passed Sgt. Whitt's hooch I glanced out over the horizon as something flickered and caught my eye. I danced back a few steps and saw what looked like a flickering light against the trees.

"Joe, look at that. What the hell is that light?"

"Ya got me, G. Looks like some kind of flame from something."

I slapped Joe's shoulder as I motioned for him to follow me, and headed down between the hooches towards the light.

"Hey, G, where the hell are you going? We got no weapons, no jackets, no helmets, and no goddamn bodies to help us," said Joe as he caught up and grabbed my shoulder, bringing me to a halt. "You go down there you're goddamn crazy! I'll go get some help."

I smiled as I got out a cigarette and motioned for Joe to light me up.

"That light is down there by the tombs and ten-to-one it's Diff sitting down there burning a candle for Mo. Why don't you head up to the club and grab us a six-pack. I'll go down and see how he's doing."

"Shit, ya know I bet you're right," chuckled Joe as he flipped open his zippo and lit my cigarette, then one for himself. "How'd you get so goddamn smart all of a sudden?"

"Not from hangin' around your Italian ass!" I said as I pushed my cover back on my head and blew a smoke ring back in Joe's face.

"You should be so goddamn lucky. If you ever need a blood transfusion, I'll get'um to put some of this good Italian blood in ya'...the women will never let you alone!"

"Well, I'd love to stay and bullshit with you, Mr. Scalia, but our buddy is waiting. You gonna get the brew or stay here and keep patting yourself on the back?"

"Yeah, yeah...go ahead. I'll be right down."

We separated and I moved towards the flickering light, watching as it danced off the tree limbs and metal roofs. As I got closer I could see the gray stone tomb surrounding a small candle, like a giant walled fort surrounding a small tent.

Throughout our entire compound there were probably fifteen or twenty of these tombs, built by the Vietnamese to bury and commemorate their families and loved ones. They were usually huge monuments surrounded by a three foot wall taking up about one or two hundred square feet. The monument at the center was a tall temple-like structure with pillars supporting a fancy sculpture. The artistry carved into each piece of stone brought color and meaning to the cold grayness of each rock.

Most of the time we didn't really pay much attention to the structures, we just stayed out whenever possible just to show our respect. But believe me, in many a firefight it was nice to take cover behind a huge piece of real rock rather than some old tree or wooden hooch.

As I approached the entrance of the low three foot walls, I watched as the flickering light of the candle magically danced up and down the surfaces surrounding it. Diff was sitting behind the candle leaning to one side, propped on his hand, just staring at the flame, his Maryland flag draped over his shoulder.

As I moved over beside him, I could see Mo's state flag folded and wrapped military style, lying beside the candle, symbolic of the ceremony Diff was playing in his mind.

"Hey, pal, you okay?" I whispered as I knelt down beside him. I lit another cigarette off of mine and handed it to Diff as I took my cover and laid it down beside his.

"They killed my black buddy, G," whispered Diff as the flame of his cigarette lit up the tears on his face. "They blew away one of the nicest guys I've ever known."

"Yeah, I know, pal. You couldn't get any better than Mo. He

cared about all of us." I put my hand on his shoulder as we both stared at the light.

"There's so goddamn much shit out there that doesn't deserve to live, why take away my buddy?" His voice quivered as he took deeper drags of his cigarette. "I hate this fuckin' place. And I hate this fuckin' war. Why does someone like Mo have to die for this place, the armpit of the world?" Diff flicked his cigarette against the wall as Joe came walking in with six cold beers under his arm.

Joe glanced at me and rolled his eyebrows up as if asking me if everything was okay. I shook my head yes as he sat down beside us.

Joe took off his cover and tossed it with ours as the three of us encircled the burning candle, starring at its flame as if mesmerized by its movement. He opened three beers and handled each of us one.

"Here, Diff, let's drink one for Mo."

We spent the better part of the next hour saluting our fallen friend and cursing the stupid war. As we finished the last of our beer, the candle slowly burned away to nothing as the flickering light turned to black against the walls. We made our way back up to our hooch in a silent march, in silence for Mo.

> *The papers, radio, and news are plastered every day with talk of the war and talk of the casualties. They say we're not winning, but we're staying well ahead – is that all that counts, just staying ahead? I get away from it all by driving out Scenic Highway and just parking by the beach. That's where we'll meet…I'll see 'ya there G-Man…*

It was great hearing the sound of the future and what lies ahead; it's great that someone else questions our cause, yet praises our heroics; it's great hearing her words of encouragement after hearing nothing all day but the sounds of death.

THE LOSS OF A FRIEND

The next day came ever so quickly as most of us tossed and turned our way through the nightmare of what had happened to our friend. As we gathered at the mess hooch for breakfast, the silence of the morning was commemorative of how we felt on this day after.

Lieutenant Barton and I were up early and ready to hit the chopper earlier than usual hoping to spot the remnants of any enemy activity from the night before. The morning dew glistening off the jungle roof seemed to signal a new day to the clouds and sky above, a new day for most of us, but unfortunately not for all of us.

Our chopper swooped low passing over the area where the enemy mortar fire had originated. We immediately spotted a small group of troops in the area, and recognized them as friendlies that had been sent out in the wee hours of the dawn. They waved feverishly as we approached, I'm sure to let us know immediately that they were on our side.

We didn't spot any movement that morning, but did plot quite a few new coordinates to hit each night, coordinates that looked like new paths of infiltration that the VC had maybe been using. It was these routes that supplies were leaving North Vietnam and traveling through our territory to reach the units of enemy troops down south. We had to hit them hard and constantly patrol the area for sightings and tell tale signs.

As we arrived back at camp from our reconnaissance mission and were unloading the chopper, Sgt. Whitt caught up with me.

"How'd the flight go, G?"

"No problems," I answered as I threw my radio gear on my back.

"We spotted some suspicious areas a little west of here, so we'll send some ambush patrols out tonight to some and pound the others with arty."

"Sounds good. By the way there's a six-by going down to DaNang at noon today to pick up medical supplies and weapons, we're gonna send Mo's body down on that. Diff's drivin' and thought maybe you and Joe would like to be his radio escort in the jeep. What do you say?"

"You got that right," I said as I smiled in appreciation, not happiness.

"Okay, I mentioned it to Joe and he's getting the jeep ready, so just let me know when you're ready to take off."

"Okay, Sarge…thanks!" I gave him thumbs up motion as I grabbed my hard-hat and headed back towards the hooch. I knew Joe would be fixin' up the jeep and checking out the radio gear, so I just needed to stow this gear and get my traveling clothes on.

As I left the hooch and was standing by the water-buffalo filling up my two canteens, Lt. Barton was coming back from the FDC after filing our plottings for tonight.

"You look like you're headed somewhere, G, what's going on?" he asked.

"Sarge is sending a truck down to DaNang to pick up supplies, so Joe and I are escorting him down in the jeep."

"Not today you're not, I need you ready for a patrol we're settin' up for this afternoon, and he'll have to get somebody else."

"But I wanna go on this one, Lieutenant. We're escorting Mo's body down to be sent home," I said as a chill went over my body just saying it.

"Sorry, G, but you're my RTO (radio-telegraph operator) and I need you in the field today, you'll have to let this one go without you. I know this means a lot to you, Joe, and Diff, but we all need to get it together and move on, okay?"

"Okay, I'll let Joe and the Sarge know. What time we leavin' today?"

"Let's say about 1300 hours. Let the rest of the group know to muster at the chopper pad at twelve thirty, okay?"

"Okay, Lieutenant," I said as I capped the second canteen and headed towards the motor pool area to tell Joe and Diff about the change of plans. He slapped me on the shoulder as he left, knowing what this trip meant to all of us, but also knowing he needed our experience on his patrol.

I caught up with Diff and Joe over at the motor pool getting the two vehicles ready for the trip down south.

"Hey, guys," I said as I approached them from behind, spreading my arms and slapping them both on the back, "I can't make it."

"What the hell you mean you can't make it?" snapped Joe as he spun around to face me.

"The Lieutenant grabbed me for a patrol today at 1300 and I gotta' be his radio."

"Aw shit!" Diff said as he took the cigar butt out of his mouth and spit to the ground. "Did you tell him what was happening here?"

"Yeah, yeah. You know how he is. He knows what this means to us, but he wants experience out there with him today, not some green radio man. I gotta' go with him…no choice."

"Okay," said Diff. "I'll see if Mike or Lenny wants to go in your place. Won't be the same though."

"Yeah I know. Gimme a beep before ya' leave; I gotta go in and tell Sarge about the change in plans," I said as I went up the steps into the motor pool hooch.

It wasn't too long after that I heard the roar of a truck engine and cut off my conversation with Sgt. Whitt to go outside. I was walking out the door just as Diff and Joe were climbing into the cab of the truck and Ron was starting up the radio jeep.

"I see you guys found a replacement for me," I yelled as I jumped down the steps and waved to Ron.

"Yeah, I was heading for Mike's hooch and ran into a real life volunteer. Couldn't keep him away," said Diff as he tipped his hat to Ron who was laughing his head off in the jeep.

"Shit, Ron, you should have learned your lesson by now about volunteering for anything in the Marine Corp," I yelled as Ron started the jeep, adding more noise to the already loud sound of engines.

Ron was laughing and waving as he called in to the FDC for radio contact and alerted them that his convoy was about to leave the compound.

"Hey, Ron, ya' ready?" shouted Joe as he hung his head and rifle out of the side window.

Ron gave thumbs up and put the jeep in first gear as he sputtered off. The truck started off after him as Diff and Joe gave us thumbs up and headed down the compound road. Sgt. Whitt and I saluted good-bye as the truck passed carrying Mo's body in the back.

"See ya', pal!" I muttered as a lump formed in my throat.

The dust trailed after them as they drove down the entrance road and headed out of the compound gate.

It seemed like ages ago that our trucks were coming through those gates as we motored into Phu Bai for the first time. I can see Mo's face as he poised at the top of a six-by truck, standing behind an M-60 machine gun. "Aw right! This is my kinda' place, real houses and all!" he yelled as his pearly whites gleamed with excitement.

Mo was the kind of guy who scared you to death to look at him because of his size and muscular build, but his heart was the biggest part of him. He was really gentle as a baby…if you knew him.

I watched for a second as the truck with his body drifted down the road. Even after he was gone a few days, it would still be hard for us to go to his hooch and not see him sitting in the same old chair of his, writing a letter home or shuffling a deck of cards. Later, we would eventually go through his belongings and gather everything to send home to his family. As part of that chore, we all joined in to write a joint letter to his family, letting them know our feelings and sorrow. So many times you hesitate doing something like that for fear you'll stir up feelings that the family can't cope with—but it really turns out to be a cherished keepsake and memento that the family remembers him by. We wanted his mom to know the kind of man he was and that he died in the line of duty helping others. So many times the immediate family is just told the bare facts—killed in action—

period. It means so much to know some details. Mo was a true Marine, in the fullest sense of the word, one hell of a man, one hell of a friend and comrade.

As Sgt. Whitt and I turned to head back in the hooch, an explosion rang out thundering successive shock waves throughout the camp.

"Oh shit!" said Whitt as we jumped off the steps and looked up the road in the direction of the clouds of dust drifting off to the side.

We could see the truck stopped just outside the gate and ahead of it were clouds of black smoke rising from the jeep.

We took off running up the road, both empty-handed, not even caring that we didn't have any weapons, helmets, or any protection. We were more concerned about our comrades than our safety. We arrived ahead of everyone else in camp who were running down the road. What we found was disaster facing us again!

Joe was kneeling about ten feet away from the jeep with Ron laying on the ground beneath him. Diff was on the PRC-25 backup radio in the truck calling for a chopper for med-evac and support.

I ran over to Joe as he jumped up to get the first aid kit out of the truck.

I looked at the jeep that was a shriveled up mass of twisted metal—Ron had no doubt hit a land mine that had been planted in the road overnight outside of our entrance.

I knelt down beside Ron and picked him up in my arms as he started to choke from the blood in his mouth. I could see he was really tore up bad, especially in the legs and groin area. The blast had detonated right under him and blown through the jeep bottom right up to him. It was amazing he was even alive at all.

Blood was everywhere as Sgt. Whitt and Joe tried to wrap what was left of his legs with gauze wrap.

"Where's the goddamn bird!" Joe screamed as tears rolled down his blood smeared face.

Ron opened his eyes and looked at us as we tried to comfort him as best we could.

"Water…I can't breathe," he whispered a he licked his lips with his tongue.

"Diff, throw me a canteen," I yelled as I propped Ron's head a little higher against my leg so he could swallow easier.

I gave him a small drink. "Easy now, pal, not too much."

His eyes were darting as I could see the color rush from his face.

"Hold on, Ron, a chopper's on the way," I assured him as I threw the canteen aside.

"Hey, guys, do me a favor," Ron whispered in a low straining voice. "Don't let them just send a damn telegram to my wife about me…make sure they send someone around…not just a cold dry telegram."

"Take it easy, buddy, you're not going anywhere," said Joe as he knelt on the other side of Ron.

"G,…tell Laura and Kathy…I love them dearly…please tell them," Ron quivered as he gasped for each breath. Blood was coming out of the corners of his mouth.

"Okay, pal," I said as the tears were streaming out of my eyes blurring my vision completely.

"G,…especially my little girl…Kathy…I'll never see her again…my little Kathy…"

A tear streaked down his bloodied cheek as he sighed a final breath. There was silence.

He was gone!

I couldn't believe it. We all burst into tears.

As the chopper hovered in the distance, we each hugged his blood-tattered body as we laid him down to the ground. Our buddy was gone. Taken from us!

Diff jumped out of the truck cab and got so pissed off he reached down to his belt, yanked out a hand grenade, pulled the pin, and heaved it down the road as far as he could. It exploded with a thunderous impact as we all treated it as a tribute to our fallen comrade.

The medics tried to work on his body but we knew, and they knew, it was just a routine exercise. They lifted him onto a stretcher and carried him to the chopper as we stood limp and stunned, watching helplessly.

As the chopper took off and was gone in the distance, we stood together as one. Again we had suffered a loss. But why?

It would take several weeks for the memory of what had happened to our two friends Mo and Ron to leave our foremost thoughts. Mo was one of our closest buddies regardless of whether he was black, white, or green. Prejudice had no place in a war and it was something rarely confronted by any of us. I didn't care what color the man to my right was just would he protect my right side as I would protect his left; would he give his life for me as I would his.

Ron's death was no less dramatic, especially for me. I was supposed to be in that jeep. I was the one scheduled to take that trip to DaNang. My life should have been taken, not his. But it wasn't to be...I was here and he was gone. How is that decided? Many times I walked over to the twisted wreck of that jeep, staring at the mangled mess, wondering why him and not me. I couldn't answer that question, but regardless, I had lost a close buddy. My comrade had died in my arms and it was devastating. Comradery was part of a war, the part you liked the best...the only part you liked.

> *You often mention your buddies over there; they sound like a great bunch of guys. Do you read each others mail – do they know me? It sounds like you really have a family away from home. I can tell they mean a lot to you. Give them my love...*

Night was upon us again and we were pressing a few cans to our lips as we usually did at the end of each day. It was a sad time because so much of our camp had been destroyed during the shellings, and most of all two of our dear friends had perished under our eyes. Drinking beer was not a celebration but an escape for us. It was a way to put aside the hard facts of this day and put our young minds back into gear and away from the horrid events of the day.

I had FDC watch on this night so I didn't drink much and decided to hit the sack early. I knew two in the morning would roll around real quick and with the enemy action as heavy in the area as its been, I knew it would probably be a busy night.

"See ya' later, guys, I'm gonna hit it early."

"That's right, you got watch tonight, don't ya?" said Diff as the little stump of a cigar in his mouth shook with every word.

"Okay, G," waved Joe, "keep those damn slant eyes out of this area tonight, I got a hot date with my girl on the beach. And let me tell you, she is just crying for me to get in her pants. But, being the considerate gentleman that I am, I have respected her so far. But tonight—I'm gonna throw her some meat. Tonight she meets the Big Ragu!"

"Shit, who you kiddin'," snapped Diff, "you can't even spell respect."

Joe and I glanced eye to eye, jumped towards each other, put our arms around each others back, and as rhythmically as the Radio City Music Hall Rockettes, kicked our legs up one at a time singing, "R-E-S-P-E-C-T, this is what you mean to me, R-E-S-P-E-C-T, sock it to me, sock it to me, sock it to me..." Our words tapered off as we danced arm in arm right off the edge of the deck, knocking over the latest pyramid of beer cans that Jenkins and Diff were working on. We proceeded to fall down the hooch steps to the hard dirt ground below smiling brilliantly as we waved good-bye. It hurt when we hit, but the applause that echoed made up for the three beer cans that were embedded in my chest.

After picking each other up, dusting off, and tipping my hat to the crowd, I patted Joe on the rear and started walking towards the hooch which was about three down from the beer hall. As I looked up, I saw a clear calm night with so many stars in the sky it almost seemed overcrowded. The noise of the beer hall festivities drifted quieter in the distance as I walked further away into the night air. I started thinking how nice the peaceful quiet moments are here, moments so few and far between that you tend to forget this is the way it should be most of the time. This is the way it was meant to be, nature alive in a world peaceful and serene, resting comfortably after a warm uneventful day.

I can tell by your letters you're having a tough time over there. You don't talk much about what goes on, but if television and news broadcasts are showing us any kind of reality for what's over there, then I pray for you. I know at times it's hard to cope and it's hard to go on but you have to, for me. By the way, I'm getting tired of picking up 'Life' magazine and wondering if I'm staring at your picture...I want one. Now! I want a flick (as you call it). Now, I sent you one (finally after six months of your begging), so it's your turn. Please...

I went back to our hooch and immediately crawled in to grab a few hours sleep. Before I knew it Mike was shaking me to get up and get over to the control center for my watch. It didn't take much to wake me up, I've always been a good sleeper once I go to sleep, but easy to wake up when its time. I dressed and walked across the compound towards the huge sandbagged bunker situated in the center of the camp. The control center was dug in underground, then fortified with sandbags on all sides and on top, all about two to three foot thick. The only noticeable sign of what was beneath this massive mound of sand was the various antennas and wires sticking out of the top and along one side.

I reached the secured entrance and walking down four steps, turned and entered the brightly lit room. The entire center was one large open area. Radios lined one wall, each tuned in to a frequency of one of our artillery encasements, the next closest artillery base, the air field, and any patrols out in the field who may need our support. A total of ten radios were usually active at one time. The back wall was maps and charts of the entire area for about twenty-five square miles. Covering the many maps was plastic that was marked with the coordinates of positions that would be hit that night, suspected enemy movements, positions of our patrols, and all happenings in the area that we should be aware of. Four men usually manned the bunker each night—an officer, a watch leader, a radio operator, and an artillery liaison person. Our unit, having just one officer, did not usually have but three people each night, the watch leader also acted as the watch commander.

On this particular night there were only two people on duty, Lenny and Mike—we were short-handed because of losing two of our guys so it was a staggered shift. I relieved Mike for six hours; Lenny would be relieved in another three hours. I had not only radio experience, but experience in plotting positions on the map from working so closely with the lieutenant, so I usually assumed the role of watch commander juggling my duties between boards and the radios.

"Well, it's all yours, G. Nothing happening out of the ordinary," said Mike as he gathered his writing materials from the desk. "Lenny will fill you in on the board plotting for the night—have fun!"

"Okay, pal. Sweet dreams and we'll do what we can not to interrupt your shut-eye too much," I answered as I threw my junk on the desk and walked over to where Lenny was sitting.

"Hey, guy. Another night, another twenty cents in the ole pocket," joked Lenny as he swivelled around in the rickety old office chair.

"Yeah shit, I can't imagine what I'm gonna do with all this damn money I'm making over here," I said as I leaned over the maps studying the coordinates marked in red and black. "Christ, with service pay, overseas pay, hazardous duty pay, and making corporal, I'm just rollin' in money. In fact, I can smell that Corvette I'm gonna buy when I get home!"

Lenny laughed as he filled me in on the locations of our patrols and other friendly activity in the area as we both studied the massive map. We then both settled down to our nights activities which, when not plotting new positions or receiving radio requests, was spent reading the latest *Stars and Stripes* newspaper, *Playboy* magazine, or writing letters home.

I had brought my latest letter from Patty that I had received today and decided to read it a second time, which wasn't unusual, I usually read and re-read her letters two and three times.

I received another of your great letters today....you're my day-maker! I'm sorry you hadn't received my last letter when you wrote it though. I really feel bad when I don't write as soon or often as I should.

She wrote me at least every other day, if not every day, and she wasn't satisfied with herself. She wanted to give more!

I tried to write her as often as I could, usually every two days or so while at the same time writing to my parents and friends. I usually kept everyone abreast of our day to day activities, but didn't really go into details as far as patrols, assaults, bombings, or tragedies that would beset our unit. The sad and troubled times our group had been through in the last few weeks had created lasting memories in our minds that we would not soon forget—they were sad moments in our lives that we didn't care to write about or bring back to mind. I really think Patty sensed these moments and when times would get really tough it would take just a simple letter from her to make me feel that I was supporting her rather than her supporting me.

I felt pretty low all day at work today and on the way home I thought of you and how low your day must have been over there...and here I am complaining. As soon as I get home, my first chore is always to check the mail and as always you brought my mood around again. You do me worlds of good. A letter from you is almost like a 'date,' because through each one I get to know a little more about you. That's what dating is all about, isn't it? I love you already!

Each letter we exchanged seemed to build a stronger bond between us as we nursed each others wounds and prepared each other for the next days encounter with the world. I often wondered if she kept me busy keeping her busy, a ploy to help me keep my mind busy helping her. Whatever the case, I'm sure she read between the lines, and knew when the stress and strain of the war was almost an unbearable confrontation.

My watch was a fairly routine night with no major incidents and plenty of time to finish at least one letter to everybody. As my duty finished and I walked back to my hooch, the sun was beginning to peak over the horizon. The warmth of its rays were beginning to put aside the ever-so-slight chill of the night as I crawled under my poncho liner to grab a couple hours shut-eye before the heat of the day got under way. Its certainly not as easy to get to sleep now as it used to be in days past. Is a man meant to keep his sanity and sleep at night after holding his comrade while life slips through his fingers? Is man meant to sleep at night after gunning down his fellow man? Can we easily sleep when our day was spent picking up the pieces of innocent civilians who are mutilated and tortured just to prove a point? Are we expected to shut our eyes without seeing the scorched, burned, deformed bodies of children who wake up to the sounds of bombs and napalm instead of their mother's voice? Can we shut our eyes and now remember the loss of a friend? Thank God we have other things to put our minds to sleep. Thanks for Patty...goodnight, Miss Chapman!

THE LONGEST DAYS

The dog days of the war were upon us as each day was a week and each week seemed a month. The hot and bitter weather cooked our skin as daily temperatures topped 100 degrees. Even though the VC seemed to close in tighter every day, our biggest enemy turned out to be the insects, the rats, and the unmerciful weather. No one survived a patrol without a trip to the medic to be treated for bites, stings, parched dry skin, or blistered peeling feet. Our entire compound seemed to be part of the walking wounded, fighting to go on, fighting to meet another day in an endless stream of days.

We found it tougher and tougher to keep our spirits up and our minds alert. It took close comradery and team dedication to go on and embark on yet another patrol. Whereas a few months ago we had very little close contact with the enemy, out patrols fought almost daily skirmishes as the VC forces seemed to strengthen and expand. It seemed for every confirmed kill, a dozen new soldiers would be spawned off, giving us little confidence and no satisfaction.

These were the times it was hard to go on, hard to muster up the willpower and stamina to keep your eyes open without saying the hell with it; I know I'm going to die, why prolong the agony? Many nights on patrol as the late afternoon sun took shelter behind the horizon, our squad would settle into an appropriate position melded into the surroundings. As we blended our bodies and firepower into the brush we memorized our surroundings and reviewed our purpose. Our bodies would sweat more as the heat of the dry dusty jungle floor smothered our clothes and parched our lips. As the orange light of dusk turned to the black sky of night we shivered with the hope that the new dawn would lead us safely back to camp and security once more.

We would stay awake for a while as we quietly joked and remembered places we'd rather be. As the night progressed, it grew quieter as each of us rehearsed in our minds what to do and when to do it, should the time come. It happened so many times before, yet every patrol was different, each night was different. The mind wanders and creates visual fantasies, fantasies of terror and pain—it makes you cautious. You hope your buddies on each side of you are experiencing the same thing, and then they too will react quickly.

Time crawls. The glow of my watch gets stronger, but the numbers become harder to read. A branch cracks in the distance and all is silent. Your breathing stops as you swallow involuntarily. Your eyes try to push the darkness out of the way as you listen for that one telltale sign that tells you its time. But it passes, and will pass a dozen more times as the night drags on. Your night vision, aided by the moon, now outlines every tree, each branch, and each soldier surrounding you. An occasional lighter clicks, as the spark of the flint lights another in an endless chain of cigarettes, which you conceal cupped in the palm of your hand as you puff away the hours.

You know it will happen, when is the only unanswered question. Your mind begins playing the odds as you wonder if this is the patrol that others will come out looking for in the morning. So you try not to think. You remember the good things.

I can't explain how I feel. You've become such an important part of my life, it's hard to comprehend how 'we' happened. I do know that not a day goes by that you're not in my thoughts and in my prayers...

Reality snaps you back as someone sneezes. It breaks the boredom of the moment and causes a snicker of laughter to go through the squad; yet you cringe, hoping it didn't give away your presence. Another branch snaps, but you immediately know it's someone to your side re-adjusting their position—trying to keep their body from falling asleep. You pick up where you left off.

Sometimes I'm up in my room at night and I wonder to myself what you're doing right at this instant. I usually end up wishing you were right here beside me (wow, that would be nice)...now, now, Patty, let's keep it clean! Okay, I'd be happy just to have you in Pensacola...but that day will come real soon, so hang in there G...

I shutter to think what I'd be doing if I were there with her now, goose bumps cover my arms. Painfully, I light yet another cigarette as I jockey my legs into yet another cramped position, just to wait for the unknown. As I stare to my left, I can make out the outline of Joe who is nestled down between two trees, probably pretending they're two girls, a grin crosses my lips. My watch now shows three-thirty, great, only two more hours 'til daylight and the long walk home. Quietly, I begin my hourly radio-check with our command post as I inform them that all is well in jungle land. I don't dare speak to break the ever present silence; I quietly key my handset two times which is the predetermined signal that our patrol is fine.

Mosquito repellent doesn't work worth a shit. An endless stream of gentle slaps can be heard down the trail. The clearing we have chosen for tonight is at a fork of two suspected enemy trails. Movement has been sighted in this area for the past few nights and it is thought that a major tunnel system lies just to the south of this position. We've set up horizontal to the point of the fork, clearly in line to observe both trails at once.

The nights in Pensacola are as beautiful as the days – it's a town I think would suit you fine. In fact, according to the girls at work, Pensacola would welcome you with open arms! Now, now I say, only my arms....

A sound brings me back to reality as my heart skips a beat. A shuffling can be heard in the distance as movement seems to be coming this way. I try to listen harder, as if I can control the volume of my hearing. There's definitely something out there. I can feel everyone around me re-adjusting their positions as it becomes apparent to all that it isn't our imagination. The silence is interrupted by the slight jingle of ammunition as John, the a-gunner for Lenny on the M-60 machine gun, positions a clip of rounds, ready for anything.

I slowly turn my radio completely down so no giveaway sounds come from my corner of the world as I position my eyes down the barrel of my M-16 rifle. The sounds have stopped, but a slight rustling continues. The adrenaline pumps, my heart races. I shiver with fear. A mosquito is sucking the living shit out of my neck but I let him drink, I'm not moving my body. My eyes begin to ache from staring so hard.

Suddenly a shadow can be seen, then two. Are they real? They're creeping so they're real! My finger slips slowly onto the trigger as the sights at the tip of my rifle focus on the center of the shadow.

Three, four, five. God, how many more? How close will they get?

Diff was our click-man at the center of the formation just to the right of the machine gun. As soon as he felt it was right, he would open up.

Six, seven, eight, nine. Shit I hope it's a squad and not a whole damn platoon. Mangy gooks, I hate'um. Sneaky little runts! They killed Mo and Ron…

We knew Diff would wait until the last possible moment when we could get the best clean shot at the whole group, yet not let them get close enough to hear our heartbeats.

They brushed aside branches as they moved closer to the fork in the trail. They whispered quietly, unsuspecting.

As I felt the moment getting close, I reached down and keyed the handset to my radio four successive times. No one could hear anything on our end because I had turned the volume completely off, but that was our pre-arranged signal to Ladybug that we were about to make enemy contact. The FDC would pick up our signal, hopefully, and zero in on our coordinates, then alert Snoopy for further orders, should we need them.

By now the lead figure was at the fork as his ten or so shadowy followers approached in a single column. As three of them gathered at the point, I felt it was time...where's Diff, I hope he's awake. I hope everyone else is awake. My heart skipped a beat as the thought went foolishly by.

I was shaking as I positioned an extra clip next to my elbow and applied slight pressure to the trigger.

Boom!!

Off went Diff's rifle in a spurt of fire as the M-60 immediately followed his lead. Within a millisecond our twelve guns were peppering the entire trail with rapid fire. They hardly knew what hit them as the element of surprise again became the victor. Our experience as a unit had each one of us positioned to direct our own firepower at a different point in their column of men, so the entire line was met with equal impact. Hardly a shot was returned as they dropped almost instantaneously.

We stopped our fire.

The darkness was cloud-covered as the smoke of our weapons and the dust of the trail billowed in the night air. The smell of gunfire reeked as the silence was overridden by the ringing in our ears.

We waited. Nothing moved. We knew to wait in silence. We didn't want to expose ourselves to another squad that may have been following this one. These dinks usually travel in packs.

The silence was broken by a moaning from across the trail. We waited, it stopped. My eyes never left the trail, my finger never left the trigger. The sounds of new clips entering rifles could be heard as our guys reloaded with fresh cartridges.

We would end up waiting another hour with nothing moving at all. Diff had worked his way around every position and was satisfied that we had no injuries—if we did it had to be that someone shot themselves because the gooks didn't even get a shot off!

As the dawn of the morning sun rose, we came out of hiding and investigated our intruders. Thirteen confirmed dead was the headcount, no wounded. I had radioed in the results of our confrontation and we gathered up their weapons and ammo to take back with us. Off in the brush I saw a shiny glistening object that turned out to be a chrome-plated .45 caliber US Army pistol. That was my souvenir—one I would end up using during the rest of my tour of duty and eventually send home, piece-by-piece, over a month long period.

As we headed back in, with the compound in sight, we again were thankful that we had made it through yet another night. Most of the guys were just heading to the mess hall for breakfast as we strolled in, ready to just hit our racks for a few hours shuteye.

"Well, another night, another thirteen dead gooks," said Joe as we both dropped our gear beside our racks.

"Yeah, thirteen down and a million to go," I answered as I fell on my cot and moaned in ecstasy. "Have I been looking forward to this for ten hours or what?"

"Want a drink?" asked Joe as he poured a new scotch and water into his mug.

"Naaaahh," I signed. "Patty doesn't like me drinking before I pick her up."

"Oh, you got a date with Patty lined up, huh, pal?"

"You bet...Pensacola, Florida, here I come."

I was out like a light.

> *I hope your day was okay today. Sometimes I wish I could just pluck you out of that horrible country and set you right beside me here. Jean is always telling me what a dreamer I am, but I keep saying okay, someday you'll see. You better not let me down G – I hate to break dreams...*

As the weeks passed, each day brought more and more frustrations and less and less purpose to our being over here. As we would sweep through hamlet after hamlet, we were met with silence and hesitation. It's almost as if the villagers questioned whether we were really there to help, or just to cause them grief. As we swept through each area, we'd drive Charlie further back, further away from the villages. The locals seemed to appreciate what we were doing, yet completely frightened by our mere presence. It was tough because we had to be forceful with them, so they wouldn't harbor the VC behind our backs, yet gentle enough to ensure them that we did in fact care about their well-being. Many times they were caught between the two forces, VC on one side, us on the other. The VC would threaten, torture, and kill them, forcing them to hide their weapons and food inside the hamlet; yet they would deny to us that the VC had ever been in the area. They were obviously scared to death. Once we found out what was going on and that they were in fact lying to us, we had no recourse but to torch their hamlet and destroy the VC contents.

Sometimes we would torch three or four hamlets a week, as we led the women and children out to safer areas. The kids always seemed to love our presence, but the elderly and women never seemed sure. Sometimes they saw us at our worse, which I'm sure left lasting impressions on them...we all break at some point.

> *Well, what do you know; you do keep your promises. I was really excited to get your letter yesterday but to find a picture inside was fabulous (wow, no wonder the girls from home write!). You're exactly like you described and just like I pictured (uncanny, huh!), blonde, built, and good-looking (as you can tell I'm pleased). You no doubt would have no problems getting around in this town, Pensacola would welcome you! Tonight I'm taking you to bed with me... (Patty, cut that out, what will he think of you?). Oh well (yawn, yawn) it's getting late so keep up the spirits...*

As the monsoon rains of September and October hit us, it not only drenched our bodies but continued to dampen our spirits. It was a great time as all of us began counting the days until our tour of duty was up. The sad thing, of course, was actually saying good-bye to the guys, especially those of us who had been so close for so long. Mike and Lenny had left for home in August and we partied all night celebrating their 'freedom.' Diff was next to go as his days dwindled down to less than a month. He would be the next hardest for me to say good-bye to, with of course Joe being almost impossible.

The big problem with becoming a short-timer is the fear you build inside yourself that keeps you from wanting to take any chances whatsoever. The fear in us was probably a lot greater than the guys who had it the toughest, out in the field constantly, but with us being in a fairly secure artillery unit, we confronted face-to-face dangers a lot less.

You would probably think that as your time dwindled down; your morale would heighten, just thinking about being closer to going home, but no. The war sucked and we hated it. We weren't winning, we weren't even making progress. The more we killed, the more we saw!

The longer you were over there, the more you hated the gooks as each day went by. They weren't the normal enemy, they were animals. It wasn't like man fighting man, it was man fighting the early tribesman of Africa who lived by the jungle rules and had insane cannibalistic ways. To deal with man and his weapons is one thing, but to face the fear of the booby-trapped jungle and the inhumane characteristics of the VC was a hard fear to overcome.

> *I can tell by your letters that your mood is at an all time low. Well, perk up Gar – I won't have it! I want you here, and I want you now! Now if you get down in the dumps, who's going to keep my spirits high? I'm counting on you for that, Corporal Lusby, so straighten up...you're my mood, my day-brightener, and my hope. What hope you say? Well, the hope that my beach partner will do what he said he would. Come down to Pensacola and meet me on the beach, and sweep me off my feet!!*

Her words kept me going and anxious to get through these hard times and impossible circumstances.

Days before Diff was to go home, we received word that one of our patrols, sent out the night before to set up an ambush, had not returned and had not been heard from by radio since two in the morning. They were our sister unit working with us to control the area.

As the word of the lost squad spread, we were eager to help in any way we could, which included forming a patrol to find them. Joe, Diff, and I, being the senior ranking and experienced members of the unit, insisted that we be the ones who lead a patrol in search of our comrades.

Joe and I insisted that Diff not go, but he wouldn't hear of it.

"No way you're leaving me behind!" shouted Diff as he pushed everyone else aside and positioned himself at the head of the column. "I'm in charge and that's it!"

We knew we couldn't talk him out of it. When it came down to helping a fellow Marine he was first in line, short-timer or not. Sgt. Whitt certainly wasn't going to order Diff to stay back; he would rather have Diff's experience out there anyway. So it was settled!

As the light of morning filtered through the hot tropical dew of the night before, it revealed a day of scorching heat and blinding sun. As we marched out of the perimeter, the jungle was thick and wet with a tropical moisture engulfing each leaf we brushed aside. In a matter of moments, our fatigues were wet with the perspiration of the upcoming heat and our feet and trousers were engulfed in the mud and muck of the soil that once was sand but now was a rain-soaked river bed.

We walked in silence as we dug our way deeper into the terrain of the forest. Only the occasional slap of a hand could be heard as one of us swatted at yet another Vietnamese mosquito or insect. The insects in this country were a bitch; they had either not eaten in twenty years or just loved the taste of American blood. The worse for us were the mosquitoes, ants, and leeches, all of which flourished in this tropical climate. No matter how much insect repellent you used they just loved your hot sweaty body, and the same with the blood-sucking leeches. They were a pain especially in the jungle while trying to wade through the rice paddies and tall elephant grass; they'd clamp on to you, and just suck you dry. Probably the biggest pain for me were those damn red ants; they'd get inside your fatigues and just bite the ever loving shit out of you. You'd usually have to get someone to help you get the damn ants off or just drench yourself in water.

A slight fog from the morning still encased the thick brush as we slowly followed our point-man Diff through the trail of soft grey footprints. As we headed further west towards their assigned position we encountered our first intruder. Diff spotted some movement through the dense fog and raised his fist to stop the squad, positioning us low to the ground. Out of the bush meandered a small drab peasant man carrying a brown sack over his shoulder. He immediately dropped the sack to the ground and threw his arms over his head yelling "Me no VC, me no VC!"

We all slowly got up as Diff walked over to him and moved aside the opening to the sack with the barrel end of his rifle. Seeing that it was full of fruit and rice Diff motioned for him to pick it up and move along.

"Di di mau!" Diff yelled. "Di di mau!" which was Vietnamese for go quickly or get the hell out of here.

The elderly man yanked up the sack in one swoop and waddled away so fast he was gone in a second. We lined back up, spread out, and again continued our trek further into the jungle. Our squad maintained its combat formation as we picked our way through the thick green vegetation, moving ever so slowly and cautiously. After about forty minutes of thick underbrush, sludgy mud, and my shoulder-breaking radio pack, we decided to pull up and grab something to eat since we had skipped breakfast in the morning. We clustered into two groups on each side of one small clearing. I quietly radioed Ladybug that we were stopping and opened my backpack for some good ole C-rations. Using my trusty Marine Corp issue P-38 can opener I skillfully pried open the first tin that contained processed ham and eggs, complimented that with a peanut butter and jelly on crackers, and rounded the whole thing off with a mouth-watering tin cup of ice cold cocoa. Aaaahhhh, just like Howard Johnson's! My stomach groaned in agony!

After gathering our thoughts, and burping our grief, we headed down the trail towards our objective. Within about fifty yards of the ambush coordinates we started smelling smoke as a foul odor seemed to drift with the flow of the hot dusty air. We grouped together and decided to spread out horizontally to sweep the area as not to get ourselves caught in an ambush by surprise. A strange mood seemed to capture all of us as we sensed something in the area was just not right. Moving into the direct area that out night patrol had been set up in, we could see scattered weapons, ammo, and backpacks lying all over the ground. We stayed back out of the small clearing that led to a path which was the suspected enemy route that the ambush was set up for. As we crouched low to the ground, Diff and Sgt. Whitt headed into the clearing as we covered them from all sides. It was strange. In the center of the clearing was a pile of rubble that had been burned—it almost looked like the remains of clothing or rags or some kind of canvas. It was giving off an awful odor. The area immediately surrounding the clearing was void of any movement or sounds.

"Oh my god!" The first words were spoken by Sgt. Whitt as he sifted through the scorched residue. "This looks like fatigues have been piled up and burned. That stinkin' odor is the smell of leather boots burning. What the hell is going on here?"

A cold shiver went down my spine as I tried to imagine what could have happened and why the burning clothes and boots were here.

They gathered together the few weapons lying around and we grouped back together to figure out our next move. It was apparent there were no gooks in the immediate area or we would have forced them out or ran into them, unless there was a tunnel system hidden somewhere. We decided to continue to sweep the area for at least another half mile concentrating on locating a tunnel entrance or signs of which direction they were moving in.

As we edged our way through the woods, we were even more alert as we could feel the coldness of the surroundings, even on this hot muggy morning. After fifty yards or so we slowed down even more as the quietness was interrupted by the sound of running water. Our map had shown a stream nearby and our plans were to sweep through for about another hundred yards beyond the streambed. The rushing of the water became louder and louder as we closed in on the small clearing that lined both sides of the stream. The water seemed unusually loud for such a small stream although it wasn't unusual for the current to be moving swiftly southward, just unusual for it to be so loud as if blocked by rocks or a small dam.

As we moved towards the rushing stream and slowly came to the jungles edge, horror struck us. Tossed throughout the stream, obstructing the flow of water, were bodies. The naked bodies of our lost patrol were thrown throughout the area and dotting the stream in both directions. We were struck with disbelief. We instinctively fell to our knees as we combed the surrounding area with our glassy eyes, looking for signs of life, signs of the enemy just waiting to cut more of us down. But nothing moved.

"Holy shit, look on the other side of the stream. Those goddamn sick bastards," said Sgt. Whitt as he pointed straight ahead.

There on the other side the reality of this war and the sickening uncivilized minds of these 'people' confronted us. Overlooking the body-ridden stream was a bamboo pole about six feet long and stuck into the sand of the bloodied waterbed. On top of the stake was the head of one of our guys. The son-of-a-bitches had be-headed one of the bodies and put it on a pole to greet us.

As we slowly crawled out of the edge of the brush to the streams edge we were aghast with shock and sorrow. To even add to the horrible sight, the soldiers dog tags were hanging around the pole under his head and a sign was scribbled saying "A US MARINE."

I couldn't in my wildest nightmare have put together a horror scene so sickening. A sight no human being alive should ever have to think about, yet witness in person. Hot bitter tears flooded my eyes as my shock turned to sorrow, and my sorrow turned to rage. All these guys were dead, and for what? Not one good reason could I come up with. A total waste of human life for a cause we couldn't explain and for a people who couldn't care less!

Each of us was frozen in our tracks, struck with the disbelief of what we were seeing. One by one we slowly wiped our eyes and began the task of gathering the bodies of our comrades together.

"My god I can't believe this, those inhumane bastards," said Joe as he bent over to pull a body out of the stream.

Diff crossed the stream and threw his poncho over the bamboo pole as he lowered it to the ground. "If I could just meet one of those suckin' assholes face-to-face right now. Who could be so goddamn inhuman? Fuckin' dinks..."

I walked over to Sgt. Whitt and we checked our coordinates so I could radio back to base camp for a chopper. About one hundred feet down the stream our map showed a clearing where we would be able to set up an LZ to load the bodies and transport back to camp.

We split our squad up; half of us started making our way towards the clearing, while the others remained here cleaning up the area as best we could. A job that was difficult to say the least.

> *I was looking at yet another 'Life' magazine today and some of the pictures they had in there were horrible. Pictures of bodies and soldiers ripped apart by the war – most of the time I look through the pages hoping to spot you (or who I think might be you), but this was one issue I hoped you weren't in. Please don't get any bright ideas and start your movie career now by starring in one of these Vietnam articles, a hero I don't want, a guy like you I do. Come home to me, Gar, you've just got to come home...*

We followed the wood line and stream as it meandered back and forth through the thick jungle brush. As we made our last turn leading to the clearing we started hearing the sound of voices that seemed to be whispering out loud. As we moved away from the stream and back into the cover of the jungle, we slowly moved forward, cautiously scanning every nook and cranny of our surroundings as we approached the clearing from the northern side. The clearing came into sight and our eyes quickly focused on a small group of VC off to our right on the western side of the clearing. They were dressed in black and green outfits with branches and twigs sticking out of their helmets and shirts as if that would camouflage them in the bright of the day.

We sat motionless as we watched them moving weapons along the tree line; it was apparent one gook was in charge as he hastily directed everyone to position weapons here and there. Within seconds there were fifteen or twenty of them scattered all along the edge of the jungle, all doing the same maneuvers, which seemed to be preparing the site for an ambush on the clearing.

Sergeant Whitt motioned to Joe and I as we moved closer. "Joe, you double back, get the rest of the squad, and bring them up. G, you drop back about twenty feet and radio Ladybug what's going on. I want some air support ready if we need it."

We both shook our heads as we slithered out of the area. As Joe and I knocked fists together, he headed off as I called base camp and alerted them to hold up sending the bird for the bodies that the area was insecure, and to have a gunship ready to support us. A gunship was a fully equipped attack Huey armed with rockets and machine guns.

I had finished talking with the CP (command post) when Joe and the rest of our squad came moving up the trail from behind me. Scared me shitless!

We slowly made our way back to the others and were amazed that the number of VC had tripled to about forty that we could see. They were working feverishly setting up mines, trip flares, and 30 caliber machine guns, using the downed trees as makeshift bunkers.

Sergeant Whitt motioned for us to spread out perpendicular to the edge of the clearing and dig ourselves in. We all had plenty of ammo for our rifles and Jenkins was covered from head to foot with belts of ammo for our 60 caliber machine gun, which he positioned towards the middle of us.

We had just finished digging in when two of the gooks came walking from the other side of the clearing to our left. They apparently had been checking out the ambush site from across the clearing as they walked pointing up and down the tree line. They suddenly stopped dead in their tracks and whirled around towards us as if they heard something. One of them popped off a few rounds in our direction skimming over our heads by about three feet. The other one reached for what looked like a satchel charge…that's when we opened up fire.

As the two lone gooks were cut to shreds by our fire, we swung our sights and immediately blasted the other tree line with everything we had. Our initial blast took most of them by surprise as they fell helplessly without even getting off a shot. In an instant their machine guns opened up on us as they took cover and answered our fire. We were all pumping rounds like crazy from our M-16s as Jenkins zipped through belts of M-60 rounds.

From the reaction and size of firepower being returned it looked like our squad was up against a platoon of VC, although we had cut down about half of them on our initial surprise burst. The firefight continued for minutes as rounds ricocheted throughout the woods throwing tree bark, leaves, and brush floating through the air. Most of us were behind trees and clumps of bamboo, continually plummeting the enemy position with round after round.

"G, call for some air support. We don't know what else is in the jungle over there. We can't handle another platoon of these guys alone," shouted Sgt. Whitt as he changed clips and began firing again.

I notified the CP that we were under fire and we would pop-smoke to mark our position. Their ETA was approximately three minutes as I signed off and took off my radio and dropped it alongside my position. I grabbed a smoke grenade off my belt and motioned to Sgt. Whitt that I was going to make my way over to our left side to wait for the chopper and pop-smoke. I hugged the dirt as I shimmied over behind a group of fallen trees and tall bush that I could use as cover. I was positioned with a clear shot to toss the smoke on the edge of our side to mark our position. Smoke already filled the air as the smell of rifle fire drifted above the trees.

Within a minute the sound of the Huey could be heard above the pop of the rifle fire. I pulled the grenade pin and tossed it through the trees to the wood line. Red smoke immediately poured out as the Huey swiftly came into sight approaching from the east as I had directed him. He swung in low directly head-on at their position raking the area with 50 caliber machine gun fire, making it almost seem like it was raining bullets. We slowed our fire down but could see a few VC running in the opposite direction through the brush away from the line of fire.

"Fuckin' gooks are getting' away!" yelled Diff as he crawled to his knees and moved back from the front. Joe followed him as I worked my way back from my position and joined Diff and Joe. The three of us pulled back from the rest and moved down the tree line heading back towards our fallen comrades in the streambed. We decided to spread out and cross the stream heading into the jungle on the other side. As we splashed swiftly through the ankle-deep water we were jolted as we heard the roar of the chopper make its second sweep of the enemy position. This time the Huey showed off its rocket power as it blasted the jungle edge with rocket after rocket. The explosions ripped the area apart as the popping of guns stopped with the overriding sounds of rocket power.

The three of us moved into the tree line and spread out with about fifteen feet between us. A figure came running across our left side as Joe turned and cut him in half with a burst of automatic fire. Within a second, two more dinks came running behind him, firing at everything, as their bush hats flew off their heads behind them. The three of us sprayed the area with fire as both gooks fell dead.

"Son of a bitchin' bastards. These are probably the dinks that tore our patrol to shreds!" screamed Diff as he charged the two dead bodies, firing round after round into them. The bodies jumped and jerked as each round met its mark, punching holes in an already lifeless body.

"Diff, let up!" I yelled as I ran over, grabbed his shoulder, and pulled him back. "It's okay, pal, you got'um, calm down!"

He let off the trigger as fury raced through his eyes and sweat ran down his brow. He was frozen, staring at the bullet-ridden bodies. It was his way of releasing some of the rage and frustration of what we had witnessed earlier. It made you want to attack these same bodies a thousand times to vent your anger. Your comrades are the closest thing to family that you have over here, so when one of your buddies dies it plays upon emotions that many of us have never tested before. Everyone seemed to handle the death of a friend differently—some wept openly, while others discovered that they just could not. Many, like Diff, just became bitter and enraged, while others just sank into an empty shell and didn't come out. It was tough because everyone needed buddies in Nam to survive, but many guys after losing friends were just afraid to get close to anyone again. In the field everyone put their life on the line for the next guy, it was what the Marine Corp comradery was all about. Diff had seen his comrades wasted and he poured out his emotions the only way he knew how, in anger.

"C'mon let's go," said Joe as he walked back away from us and continued on a one-man sweep.

"C'mon Diff, let's get some more gooks," I said as I slapped his arm with the back of my hand.

I put my arm around his neck as we turned and started walking to catch up with Joe, when we saw him open up fire directly to his left.

"Lai day, Lai day!" he yelled as he called into the woods for the gooks to come out.

We saw two muzzle flashes and could hear the popping of rounds but couldn't see any figures. Joe stopped firing as he grabbed his arm and fell to the ground.

Diff and I returned fire in the direction of the flashes as we raced through the brush, crouching as we fired. We reached Joe and grabbed his shirt pulling him behind a group of logs for protection. Diff continued to spray the area as I attended to Joe. He was bleeding in the upper arm but had just been grazed and seemed fine.

"I'm okay, G, just got nipped. Where's my goddamn rifle? Let's get those frigin' turkeys."

I pulled my bandana off my helmet and shoved the ace-of-spades into the pocket of my fatigues. One of the many customs of the American soldier of Nam was to wear an ace-of-spades playing card on his helmet—to the Vietnamese it signified the presence of an evil spirit. So the thought was that if you're wounded or killed, the gooks will leave your body alone for fear of the evil spirit. We'd much rather bleed to death in the field then to have them torturing or stripping our body.

I tied the bandana lightly around his wound to help with the slight bleeding and we picked up our rifles to help Diff. Rounds of enemy fire raked the log in front of us as chunks of bark flew into the air.

"See anything, Diff?" I asked as I stuck my head above the stumps.

"Yeah, two of them right over behind that pile of shit in front of us." Another burst of rounds hit our log as I threw my face down into a pile of decaying leaves.

"Okay, you two open up and I'm gonna toss a grenade," I said as I pulled one from my belt and laid down my M-16.

"You see where they are?" Diff asked.

"Yeah, I got'um, let's get those bastards!"

They both opened fire, plummeting the position with rapid fire. I crouched to my knees, pulled the pin, pumped my arm, and heaved the grenade directly at their spot. Within a second of hitting, the grenade exploded, hurling debris everywhere. We stopped firing and there was silence as dirt and leaves drifted down from above. We waited. Nothing moved.

"I hate this part! But we gotta' check it out," I said as I stared at their position.

"I'll go," said Diff. "I think you gott'um good, G. You guys cover me, I want the pleasure."

"No!" snapped Joe. "I've already been hit, I'll go. You can cover me better."

"No, I'm going," said Diff as he stood up and started towards their position.

Joe and I took aim as Diff slowly stepped his way across the battle zone. His eyes were intense and his rifle poised waist-high and ready should the slightest movement come from the brush. As he carefully circled to the side of their position we could see him lower his rifle and a smile come to his face.

"Bulls-eye, guys, first class bulls-eye!"

We got up and walked over to Diff as he pounded a new cigarette on the back of his hand and flipped open his Zippo to light up. The gooks were literally in pieces, their shattered bodies absorbed every bit of the impact of the grenade. The gooks face looked like hamburger and his legs and arms were barely attached, only thin strips of muscle joined them. Their black fatigues hung in strips from the grotesque mess.

By this time the other guys in our squad were making their way to us as we could still hear the chopper making yet another rocket sweep.

"Hey, you guys okay?" shouted Sgt. Whitt as he and Tony came up the stream.

"Yeah, we're okay, just killin' some shit-ass gooks that's all," laughed Diff as the look on his face showed contentment. Not contentment for killing, just the feeling of bitter retaliation for what these gooks had done to our comrades the night before.

We grabbed their AK-47's and all of us walked back down to the stream where most of the squad was gathered. We hadn't lost anyone in the firefight and Joe's arm seemed fine as we bandaged him up for the trip back. Sgt. Whitt had radioed back to the CP and a couple of choppers were on their way to pick us and the bodies up.

As the choppers arrived and we finished loading the bodies, the gunship could be seen hovering above us protecting us from any further incidents. We hopped on board the last bird, thankful that we had all made it okay, yet contemplating what we had just loaded into the other chopper. The bodies of our fellow Americans.

On the flight back, our squad was probably the quietest they have ever been in their entire Vietnam experience. How do you talk unless it's to say obscenities? How do you comprehend an act like this, unless you drag yourself down to their mentality? How do you go on, dear god, how do you go on...

> *I haven't heard from you in three days now and I'm worried sick (to say the least). I pray you're okay. I keep telling myself that I haven't received a letter because you can't write me daily, but when I get home from work and there's no letter, my day is shattered. I wonder how I'll get through another whole day until the mail comes again. I know you don't always have a lot of time to write but please just jot down a 'hello' to let me know you're okay. Jean is always telling me I'm too impatient, too demanding, I expect too much – I guess she's right, but then again you can't tell me anything (or so I've been told). When it comes to you I don't want to wait for anything, when I want to talk to you I want you here – remember that when you're alone...I'm always with you!*

We were walking zombies for the next few days, and, for our sake, they pretty well kept our squad out of the action while our bitterness calmed down.

As the first week of October arrived, we said good-bye to our best friend and fearless leader Ted Differman. He and I promised to get in touch with each other when we both went back to Maryland. The nicest part of him leaving was the small ceremony we held for him the day he left. He got his sergeant stripes. I was glad for that, but most of all, glad another one of us would survive and get back to the sane side of Earth.

As October finished out and November came, the lieutenant and I flew out about twice a day since the action had picked up immensely. We tried desperately to pound the VC supply routes day and night to halt their infiltration of supplies and arms to the troops down south. But is seemed hopeless, as long as they had the Ho Chi Minh Trail to use, we were beaten.

We'd capture cache after cache of weapons and supplies, ammo and food, medical supplies and clothing, but it didn't seem to make a difference. As we captured more and more weapons we could see their weaponry was improving as it was obvious the Russian government was supplying them with better and better armory to use on us. Our knowledge of battle and the US weapons superiority was obvious, but fighting in their land under these conditions almost gave them the upper hand. It always amazed me how we would move into an area, find a massive tunnel system full of supplies and room-sized sleeping quarters, destroy everything in sight including the tunnel entrances, only to re-visit the same spot a week later and find it fully operational again. It's tough to plow ahead and keep your enthusiasm and spirit up when you're continually reminded that you haven't made an inch of progress. Were we wasting our time, our lives? It seemed we would accomplish a days worth of nothing—on top of that, these were definitely becoming for us, the longest days of the war!

THE WORLD

My tour of duty was slowly drawing to a close as the end of November was upon us and Joe Scalia got his orders to go home. We turned 'his' celebration into 'our' celebration as he headed out and I became the platoon short-timer with less than twenty days and a wake-up. I remember many times throughout my life when I spent a lot of time with a particular person, whether it was a guy I suffered through classes with, or the neighborhood pals I hung around with and grew to know; I got to know these people and they were part of my life, part of me. I had made a lot of friends in the service, through boot camp, infantry training, and school in California, everywhere I went I had close friends. But Nam was different. It wasn't just lying in the next rack next to a fellow Marine; it wasn't eating and working and training beside them all day; it wasn't tipping a few beers and talking about the girls back home. It was Nam. It was a long trusting companionship and closeness. It was family. We had struggled together, suffered together, cried together, and pulled each other along. We had been to hell and back together—saying good-bye was tough. You try to treat your good-byes like you've been conditioned to treat killing, by looking on the bright side. He would have killed you if you hadn't wasted him. The bright side of Joe leaving was that he, like Diff, had made it. Thank you, God. Made it to hell and back.

Saying good-bye to Joe was like saying good-bye to a brother, only this time you really wondered if you would ever see each other again. A lot of promises are made throughout life—to your high school buddies, your college frat brothers, your service comrades—most of which you never keep. "But we've just got to get together again"...yeah sure! You never do because memories fade and life goes on.

As Joe and I embraced, we made the same promise. New York and Maryland are too damn close for us not to get together. That afternoon as I watched Joe board a chopper to head for DaNang, I waved good-bye to the other person, besides Patty, who helped me get through each day. We were always there for each other, whether it was in the hooch, in the field, or under fire, we tackled it together as one. A closer buddy I've never had. As he turned and saluted that Scalia-salute, I bid farewell with a tear in my eye. Little did I know at that time that Joe and I would get together again after the service...I'm glad that's one promise we did keep!

So, now I was next. Joe handed over to me what Diff had passed to him, and each guy had passed along for months before us, the official "short-timers stick." It was a round carved stick; about 30 inches long, with the head of a dragon-type figure at the top, and a brass cap at the bottom. It had about twenty names carved into it by each one of its previous owners throughout the final days of their tour of duty. It was traditional that the short-timer of the platoon carry the stick throughout his final days in country. Finally, it was mine. Finally!

The lieutenant and I took a break in the action one afternoon and were invited by one of the ARVN commanders to his home for dinner. We worked with him very closely for about four months and it was really his way of expressing his gratitude.

The lieutenant accepted his gracious offer and I, of course, was to go whether I wanted to or not; we couldn't insult the gracious commander. Neither of us had eaten in a Vietnamese home before, but our closest sources said just to act polite and turn down nothing. Sounded simple!

We arrived that evening and to my surprise his home was nice—I guess I expected another bamboo shanty, that's all I had ever seen over here. It was the first 'building' I had seen in twelve months that was made of concrete.

His wife and daughter welcomed us, and to our surprise they

spoke fairly good English, just like the commander. His wife was a young, very good-looking oriental woman who dressed the part of an officer's wife—no doubt she was used to entertaining the many commissioned officers who came to her house. The daughter was definitely something to behold—I'm not sure at this point if she was so damn good looking, or just the first non-peasant-looking young lady I had seen in over a year. Her hair was long and flowing and surrounded her young innocent face perfectly. She wore the traditional Vietnamese clothing, but it seemed so different on her, I guess because it was clean and pressed and didn't look like it had been slept in for six months. Just as half the population of Vietnam, she had on black silk pants, but these had long slits in the legs from the cuff clear up to the middle of her thigh. Like most oriental women she did not have much in the way of a gorgeous full body, but the lines and curves of her legs sent goose bumps down my spine!

As we sat and talked of everything except the war, which surrounded us, the commander's wife was busy preparing the meal. The two officers began to admire the collection of liquor that was stocked at his bar and commenced to fix drinks. As I sat across from his daughter, not really knowing what to say, if anything, her eyes focused on mine as if sending a message. As I met her stare, she glanced toward her father as she crossed her legs. The halves of her pants fell to each side revealing her beautiful bare legs from her spiked heels up to her mid-thigh. As her eyes returned to mine, her hand went down to her knee and she slowly ran her hand up her leg to the top of the slit in her pants. I was sweating like crazy! I'm a leg man from way back, but this was insane...she was teasing me to death and loving every minute of it.

The men continued to talk as they left the bar and walked towards us bringing me a drink. Then they returned to the bar to continue their conversation, which led them to two stools at one end, completely out of our sight.

As I glanced back towards her I lifted my drink in the air and said, "Cheers!" as I slowly gulped a huge mouthful.

After glancing towards her father again, her eyes returned to me as her hands ran back down her legs and up towards her body again. This time both hands were caressing her bare thigh as she reached the top of the slit in her pants. As her eyes focused on mine she uncrossed her legs and pulled the slit of her pants leg open revealing that she had no panties on. By now I was a basket case! I smiled as I downed my drink, my eyes never leaving her teasing activities. Before I knew it she was smiling and holding her pants leg open showing me her crotch, just enjoying the reaction she was getting from me. I had often heard about oriental torture chambers, but I never thought I'd actually be in one. Or enjoy it! Just as she ran her tongue over her lips and began moving her hips and rear in a circular motion, she moved her hand over to herself and began to rub herself moving her fingers in and out of herself. Oh God!

The conversation from the bar began to regain its volume as the two officers headed back towards the room we were in. She immediately re-crossed her legs and laughed with pleasure as she flipped her pants leg over her bare leg. Sweat was pouring from my brow as I began to appreciate more and more the oriental hospitality. It was obvious she was enjoying teasing me as the smile never left her face for the rest of the night. I think this was the first hard-on I have had in twelve months.

Our talk settled around the personal aspects of our lives rather than the war that had brought us together. Eventually, after a before dinner drink of some kind of wine, we made our way to the long table, much longer than the five of us needed. One by one the bowls of food were brought out—rice, which I could have guessed; a plate of green water plant, which looked like seaweed to me; whole fish baked in banana leaf, my problem was this fish was not cleaned, everything was there; head, scales, backbone, organs, bowels, everything; and finally a large round bowl of fish eyes, right, fish eyes. How could I possibly even look at a bowl of food that looked back at me, no less eat it! I kept remembering our sources telling us it was impolite to turn anything down…oh shit!

Luckily for us, the Vietnamese appetites are small just like their bodies, so small portions were the order of the day. I tried it all, yes, even the fish eyes, which were like rubber, and thank God I'll never have to do it again. No wonder these people look half starved and frail, eating this shit!

As we ended the night and said our thanks and good-byes, my eyes glanced back towards his daughter who was standing in the background. As I looked her way she winked, smiled, and ran her tongue across her lips. Oh great, just what I needed! As we motored back to the compound, I didn't tell the lieutenant about my adventurous evening, but did re-live that night for many nights to come!

A week before my orders were due to come, I was surprised by a ceremony held in my behalf. I was awarded a Meritorious Mast by our unit for the duties I had been performing over the past few months. Since Sgt. Whitt and Diff had left, we had gotten a lot of replacement troops, FNG's, but no E-5's or E-6's to replace them. I had really been filling in for our missing sergeant and I guess the ol' corporal impressed them enough to set me up for this honor. It was really no big deal, just a certificate of merit that went in my records; it certainly didn't do much for me at the time, but I figured maybe it would help get my sergeant stripe later on.

But finally the day arrived! We had just come back from a patrol that had us all sweaty, hot, and pissed off. A simple short-range re-con patrol had turned into a major firefight against what seemed like a regiment of NVA. Our squad lost almost half our men just on one stinking burst of fire. Cut down instantly by a damn claymore mine. We were trapped behind a rice paddy dike for about ten minutes before we called in artillery and turned around the attack.

As we dragged ourselves back into base camp, I was greeted with the news that my orders had come through. I would be going home in two days. Well glory, glory hallelujah! After I cleaned up, I immediately went over and confirmed that I wasn't dreaming, it was really true. After 393 days in this godforsaken place I was chosen as one of the lucky ones who would return home alive. It was really true.

I can't believe we've been writing to each other for almost a year. It seems like yesterday that I helped

> *put those Christmas packages together and now here it is almost Christmas again (hope you're not expecting another package!). When you really think about it, it's been a long tough year for both of us, you keeping my hopes up and me keeping your spirits up. I think we've done it...I think we've made it, Gar...*

With two days to go I had a lot to do, but one of my first chores would be to write to my family and my Patty and tell them to write no more. I couldn't believe I was writing and telling everyone to stop writing letters to me. The thing that kept me going! But this, I said, is my final letter from Nam!!

I would find out that the next few days would be the scariest days of my Vietnam life. All through my final days as an official homebound "short-timer," I continuously stayed out of trouble, stayed out of the line of fire, and stayed out of the public view. No way was I going to go through thirteen months of hell, get orders to go home, and get wasted with only hours left in Nam.

I arrived at DaNang on December 19th with what I thought would be plenty of time to make it home before Christmas. Little did I know that I would get wrapped up in the biggest mess of red tape and bullshit that I would ever see? It all began in DaNang where instead of flying out that same day I was told I would be spending the night and flying out the next day. Oh good, just what I need, another night in Nam. I'm sure I'll sleep real good tonight!

The night passed harmlessly and before too long I was being herded onto a transport plane bound for Okinawa, the staging area for troops going home from Nam. You would expect that the last thing I would be scared of would be flying out of the country, but everyone on the plane was saying a prayer as we motored down the runway and became airborne. As the plane glided off the airstrip and circled over the jungle below, my thoughts were of a gook patrol sitting in the bushes with a battery of guns just waiting for our plane to take off. But alas, our plane climbed quickly to the point that the jungle below was just a mass of green, melding together, no longer dense, no longer hot, no longer smelly, no longer a part of me. We all breathed a sigh of relief as we left the land and were over the vastness of the ocean, an ocean that best of all led the way home. We all shouted, cheered, and hugged as the tenseness that had filled the air was released upon takeoff. We had made it!

The base on Okinawa was a flurry of activity as it seemed like thousands of troops were trying to get home for the holidays. It was still fairly early in the day so I figured I'd probably leave on the next plane out that day or at least the first thing in the morning. Boy did I have a surprise coming!

The Okinawa procedure was this; three planes a day left for the states, one at eight in the morning, one at two in the afternoon, and one at six in the evening. Three times a day we would muster outside our barracks and a list of the men who would be flying out on the next flight would be called out; the rest played the waiting game. I had nine shots at getting on a plane and getting home for Christmas, after that the flights would be suspended until December 27th.

Each night spent in Okinawa was an agonizing one, sleepless nights, thoughts of home, and the unknown of the next day. Everyone was elated to be out of Nam of course, but we didn't want to be out of Nam and in Okinawa, we wanted to be out of Nam and in The World.

I spent two and a half agonizing days of hearing lists of names called for upcoming flights, but not mine. On the third and last day my name was called for the next to last plane leaving that day at two o'clock. I couldn't believe my ears, my name never sounded so good as it did being called out on that day. "Corporal Gary Lusby, Serial Number 2155870."

So, on December 23, 1967, I boarded the huge Continental jetliner that would finally take me away from this "hell on earth," and put me back on good old American soil. We settled in for our fourteen hour flight and the mood was celebration, jubilation, anticipation, and downright happiness. It was quite a different flight from the one we took over to Nam where the guys and the stewardesses were quiet, solemn, and teary-eyed; this time there were no tears except tears of joy, and the stewardesses were as happy as we were. We had such a great time on the flight it seemed to really go quickly, but I will never forget the feeling felt by all when we first spotted land.

"Look, The World!" someone shouted. "I can see the states!"

As we all rushed for a window, we could see the edge of California approaching in the distance, stretching far out of sight down the coastline. The sun was shining bright as its rays bounced off the water glistening in the rough waters. We could see sailboats racing up and down the waters' edge, their colorful sails flapping in the mid day breezes.

"Gentlemen, let me be the first to welcome you back to the United States of America. On behalf of the Captain, myself, and the entire flight crew, we're all proud to have brought you back home," echoed throughout the plane as the flight crew gave us their cheerful announcement. Everyone was excited, pumped up, and ready to finally walk on American soil again.

Even though the flight took fourteen hours, we had actually gained some time since we were flying west to east, so it was early in the afternoon when we finally landed at Edwards Air Force Base. The jubilation that took place as we deplaned was indescribable. Guys were hugging everyone in sight, kissing the ground, shaking the hand of every American in sight, and literally walking around with their arms raised, staring up at the clear blue United States sky. I'm sure this was a scene that was common to Edwards with every plane that landed from Okinawa. The uncontrollable display of thirteen months of waiting, hoping, praying, and dreaming; but now the time was finally here. We had made it! We had served out time and now we were home, ready to be welcomed, applauded, and congratulated...anything!

We not only didn't have a welcoming committee...where was any American or military fanfare at all? We were just another plane load of soldiers passing through. But we were special! We had served thirteen months of hell for our country, for the American way. What happened?! People passed us like we were discarded trash!

It was my first taste of the American attitude towards the US involvement in South Vietnam. I agreed with the question a lot of people had—why are we over there? But after the first Marine lost his life for his country, we were committed to the cause and he should be treated as any other war veteran who puts his life at stake. I wondered if anyone really cared.

Our paperwork was processed quickly, which surprised us, for once the government had its shit together. Without delay we were sent out to waiting buses to be taken to the airport for our individual flights home. I had a direct flight to Baltimore Washington International airport, but my flight wouldn't leave for another three hours so I had plenty of time to enjoy the scenery.

My first order of business once I got settled at the airport was to call home and let my parents know I had landed safely and would be coming home in a few hours. Needless to say, their tears of joy said it all as we screamed at the sound of each others voice.

"Hello, Mom, Dad…I've landed in California and I'll be home Christmas eve," I said the words I had been wanting to say for quite a long time. I think the silence lasted for minutes as we let our emotions get the best of us, but we deserved it. We had suffered through thirteen months of this war, me in Nam, and my parents here. It was certainly no picnic for them being back here waiting through thirteen months of war talk, news broadcasts, casualty announcements, and days with no mail. It seemed the odds were certainly against making it home alive or even in one piece. The war had taken its toll on all of us, but we stuck it out and WE had made it.

It had been a long, long day, and this five hour flight seemed to last forever, but for some reason I just couldn't sleep…I wonder why? As I landed at the airport and we taxied to the terminal, my thoughts went back to fourteen months ago when I had arrived at the airport and said good-bye to my parents—bound for Vietnam. I remember my mother waited in the car in the parking lot because she couldn't stand to walk me to the gate and see my plane leave. Of course, my father wasn't crazy about it either, but he wasn't going to admit that. "Take care of yourself" is all we could manage to say to each other as we embraced for what could have been the last time. But, thank God it wasn't and here I was about to meet them where we had left off then.

It was a moment we all had dreamt about for a long time. We said it again and again in our letters, our conversations, and our prayers. The reunion was fantastic and lasted for thirty whole days.

I spent most of my leave languishing as a part-time civilian. Getting re-acquainted with my relatives and friends was the easy part; keeping conversation out of Vietnam was the impossible part. Suddenly, half my friends were jerks! Wanting to know "How was it really over there?" "How many people did you kill?" and my favorite one, "Did you ever have any real scares while you were over there?" Jerks! The whole freaking ordeal was a real scare. And who cares how many I killed, I was here and that's all I wanted to admit to. Suddenly, they were infatuated with the war and I was infatuated with life!

Before long I was becoming so overwhelmed with the war questions I began to avoid most of my friends. It wasn't that I was afraid to talk about the war, it's just that I needed a break, some room to breathe. Most of the time when I was out with a group of people or at a party I'd end up getting pissed off as soon as the talk got to Nam and "Why the hell we were over there?". Before too long I'd be one-on-one defending our stand in Nam—not so much that we shouldn't have been over there in the first place, but supportive of the job we were doing and how badly the people back here needed to back our guys over there. The point was always wasted though. These people just see an ugly war, in a foreign country, for no reason, and immediately shut out anything and anyone who has anything to do with the cause. I'd just like to plop their ass in a rice paddy for about an hour, surrounded by who knows what, not wanting to move for fear you'll trip a mine or see the flash of a muzzle pointing in your direction. Then we'll see what kind of support we get for our vets. Jerks, all my friends were jerks!

With the war still surrounding me everywhere I went, I finally admitted that I needed some help...and who else could give me that help and support but the one who had done it for a year, Patty. I promised her I'd call and I had waited long enough!

The adrenaline pumped through my body as I dialed the long distance number to Florida. As the numbers clicked over, I could feel a lump in my throat as my excitement began to surface. Finally, after writing for a year, we were about to talk for the first time.

The number clicked over...rang...and someone said "Hello."

"Hello, is Patty there?" I asked.

"This is Patty."

Oh my God, it was her, I couldn't believe it.

"Patty, this is Gary calling from Baltimore."

"Gary...my Gary from Vietnam...I can't believe it, you're home safe, and we're finally talking!"

From that point on, for the next hour, we never stopped talking. We had often wondered if we'd feel strange or be lost for words, but the answer was definitely no. I could have listened to her talk for hours and hours. That cute feminine southern voice with that long southern drawl just had me in a daze. Yet she was the one who commented about loving to listen to my northern accent. Just as in written form, we seemed infatuated with each other, hardly pausing to take a breath.

We finally said our good-byes and promised to begin writing again as soon as I had a new address...our plans for a beach rendezvous would continue on schedule. I felt fantastic! Not one time had our conversation been centered on Nam, the war, or anything negative. We talked of us, our letters, the names of our friends that we had written about, and our lives. My conversation with Patty did exactly what I knew it would do; calm me down and make me realize how lucky I was and how much I had to look forward to. She was again my salvation, my realization, and my medication, in a world I was unhappy with. It was so unfair to be judged by a rebellious people who are living in a capsule of solitude. A people who criticize their world and curse their fellow Americans. Jerks!

Before I knew it, my thirty days were at an end and my orders had me spending my last eight months at Camp Lejeune, North Carolina...excitement unlimited!

As bad as it sounded though, North Carolina suited me fine because it had one big plus—I was on the east coast and only six hours from home. Knowing that, I took some money that I had saved up and bought a new 1968 Dodge Charger and decided to drive down and try and make as many weekends home as I could. Little did I know that I would ultimately make it home every single weekend for eight months, except one.

I was assigned to a radio-telegraph unit and "eagerly" reported, ready to give just eight more months to Uncle Sam's cause. I spent about eight days with my new unit before the word came down that they needed instructors at the rifle range and were looking for someone with experience. Since I had just returned from Nam and had experience as not only a rifle expert but a pistol expert, they decided I was their man. My name was submitted for the job and to my surprise I not only got the job, but my sergeant stripe to go with it. A small ceremony was held the following day in front of the barracks where I was given my new stripe. Sergeant Lusby, that sounded good.

I was a little hesitant about the duty, feeling that I really didn't want to get back into the "weapons and shooting" bit this soon. I just wasn't sure I wanted to face that every day again, yet. But then I started thinking about the other side of the coin—if I could use my experience and skills to teach these future Marines how to care for, use, and respect their weapon; it would be for everyone's good...especially my fellow comrades who were still in Nam and may have some of these guys by their side. So, the rifle range it was!

I spent eight hours a day on the range teaching groups of Marines the proper way to shoot a rifle, in this case the M14 and M16 rifle. The range was a busy place with units scheduled every week to qualify their weapon. Most of the units were either new recruits out of Parris Island boot camp who were at Camp Lejeune for their two weeks of Advanced Infantry Training (ITR), or Marine Corp

Reserves from various parts of the country on their annual "summer camp" and required to qualify with a rifle every two years. Each group would spend a week at the range under our instruction, and work their way towards the last day when they would have final qualification. They would qualify as either a marksman, sharpshooter, or expert, according to their total score of firing.

The recruits were always the most fun because they were so scared to death after finishing twelve weeks of boot camp, that when a sergeant approached them, they froze in their tracks. They even tried to salute us! It was always fun to still treat them like little boot camp boys rather than Marines—we all went through it, so now it was my turn to be the bad guy. But above all, they were scary. Give a scared recruit a loaded rifle and you take your life in your hands. So my primary job was not only to teach these future jarheads to fire a weapon accurately, but to have respect for the weapon, as well as, respect for my life and the lives of others on both sides of them.

All in all it was pretty good duty and the weekends were mine, so making it home was great. I usually pulled weekend duty on base every fourth weekend, but it usually wasn't hard to sell it to someone else who was going to be there anyway.

I returned from the rifle range after a long morning of new recruits, and could see as I approached my bunk a letter had arrived. A smile came to my face as I knew just by the size and shape of the envelope that it was a letter from Patty. Sure enough, my new mailing address had caught up with me and for the first time again in weeks, mail call was my favorite part of the day.

I shoved the unopened letter under my pillow and decided, as always, to savor the joy of reading it to when the grueling day of training was over. It was still the nicest part of the day to sit down with a drink and just plain enjoy a letter from someone you care about.

Her letter was dated January 31, 1968, and it was fantastic seeing those beautiful words staring me in the face again.

> *I worried about you until I got your phone call, but when the phone rang and you said hello, my prayers were answered. After our chat – well, you were right. It was as though we'd talked a million times before. None of that strained silent stuff – notice that? The people who adamantly swear that 'you can't tell anything about a person from a letter' are all wet. We're proof!*

She said it all, we were like family that had always known each other and had only been separated by time. We talked on the phone so freely and openly, and it seemed all the promises we made each other were coming true. We had, in fact, pulled each other through a war and now it was time to get on with our plans. The Marine Corp was going to hold things up for a while, but as soon as eight months were over, Pensacola here I come. So, in the meantime we were back to the written word, something neither of us had a problem with.

> *Gary, so much has happened to me the past month or so, I hardly know where to start. Someone called me last week and said 'What have you been doing lately?' I had to say 'Well, everything, or almost everything.'*
>
> *If you recall my Winter Haven letter, you'll no doubt remember the fella I mentioned at the end (the dopey druggist, Don Wilson). Well, upon my return we became inseparable. Either he was over here every night or else we went out. We liked each other a great deal but above all we were 'friends.' Two nights after I talked to you on the phone, Don asked me to marry him. Without hesitation, I agreed.*

Wait...this wasn't happening to me. Where's Joe when I need him? I lowered the letter and laid it on the bunk without reading any further. I lit a cigarette, poured a fresh drink, and wiped the faint blur that seemed to be in my eyes. What was going on here?! I tried to ponder the sad times I had been through in Nam and the many friends I had lost in combat. I began wondering if I was now being punished for being so lucky, for traveling to hell and back.

I sat still, seated on my foot locker with my arms in my knees, staring at the floor. Was it just words on a written page to get me home safely, to keep my spirit and will up long enough to get me home? To be chalked off as a pen pal? I returned to the letter.

> *After having time to think sanely, I realized that you and I may have the makings of such a bond. Then too, I reasoned that you are (especially now!) a very good looking, freedom lovin' guy whose thoughts of marriage and the like are far, far in the future. Don was, well there's no getting around it, here and his feelings and intentions were very now. What more can I say, Gar?*

I again put the letter down, shaking my head in disbelief. It all seemed like a bad dream. We had expressed our thoughts and feelings to each other so many times, written on the pages and between every line. It seemed we were meant to be. So many times she had said we were so alike it was uncanny, we knew each other, and loved each other.

I puffed on my cigarette as I suddenly became bitter and doubting. Was the whole thing just a hobby, an assignment for extra credit – pick a G.I., write to him in Vietnam and do your good deed for America; give him hope and help him through the war and home again.

No! I couldn't believe it, I couldn't be bitter. That was not Patty. She had no obligations, she had no ill intentions, it wasn't a game, a put-on.

I poured another drink and sank further into silence and disbelief. I thought so many times of the guys in Nam that received that *Dear John* letter that put them over the edge. That one letter that tore apart the strings that attached you to that someone special back home. Unfortunately, when the strings were cut, a small piece of you dies also. I continued with her letter.

> *Fate it seems, has guided our relationship all along. Now, it seems we're being thrown apart. At any rate, it can't be changed or ignored.*
>
> *But Gar, I would still love to meet you face to face! I feel very close to you and although its not as 'close' a feeling as once I expected, I would still love to talk to you, see you.*
>
> *The wedding is set for June. Please, Gary, if at all possible, come. Don and I are buying a home in Belvedere Park and so we'll have time and room for you anytime your plans include Florida. At any rate, let me know!*
>
> *Love you as always...Patty.*

I folded the letter and threw it on my rack, lit another smoke, and made another drink. By now a few of the guys were returning from chow and the club as darkness had set in.

"Hey, G, we're headin' over to the club for a few drinks, you comin'?" said Bill as he tossed his cap on the rack. "Got a letter from home, huh? Is it Nam mail or now mail?"

"No, it's now mail," I said as I grabbed my cigarettes, drink, and cap and headed out the door. "No, you guys go ahead without me, I'm just going for a walk."

"You okay, G?" asked Terry, my Bunkie.

"Yeah, I'll make it, thanks. Just need some thinkin' time."

I buttoned my shirt as I walked out to the road and crossed to the other side. The sun had just set and there was a deep red tint to the sky just above the horizon. I walked slowly to the rifle range where I sat on the hill overlooking the empty target pits. As I stared at the smoke rising from my cigarette, I tried to piece together what had happened. We had come so far and it had been so long, why was fate not letting us meet?

I wondered what my next letter would say. How do I reply to a letter that has devastated my life? I'm not saying this was a matter of life or death and I couldn't go on—but this person was a part of me. When all else failed me in Nam, she was there. When my buddies were being blown to shreds and I was pinned down in a rice paddy wondering when my turn would come, she was there. When there was just nothing to look forward to and no one to talk to, she was there. How could I so easily forget that? How could I just accept the fact that fate had dealt another hand and now there was nothing we could do about it? Bullshit! The weddings in June—I won't give up!

I had made up my mind to write back and talk to her the best way I knew how, through our letters. I knew I wouldn't be able to sleep without getting it done, so I headed back to the barracks to start writing. I hoped most of the guys would still be at the club or the movie so I could have some time to myself to do this right. When I got back, I had the place to myself.

I thought I had written some real tough letters overseas, but this one kind of took the cake. After about half an hour of getting started, I was finally able to say what I wanted to. I basically just asked her to at least give us a chance to meet and tell ourselves face-to-face that it just couldn't be. It was so unfair to come all this way just to cast it aside for nothing. Granted, we had our friendship and memories, but we deserved more, out time spent together deserved more. Simple and to the point! The ball was in her court.

I mailed the letter the next morning, a Tuesday, and really didn't expect to get an answer for at least a week. That was the tough thing about mail now, you really just answered mail as you got it, not like before where you wrote feelings and emotions instead of questions and answers.

I went home for the weekend as I always did, and although I was tempted to call her and talk things out, I really wanted to give her a chance to answer my letter. I wanted to see how she felt now, after a week or so to think. Nothing arrived Monday, but on Tuesday I had a letter waiting for me when I got off the range.

Hi Gar, it was great to hear from you, especially after my last letter. Just like your letters from Vietnam I could sense your feelings in each of your words. Gar, I'm really sorry it turned out this way; I know it's not fair, but like you've said many times, life never is fair. I spent a lot of time thinking things over this week and trying to convince myself (and others) that I was making the right decision. Throughout the week I was bombarded by comments and criticisms from the family as to your chances. My biggest competitor was Jean (we always have talked so openly to each other, she's like the big sister I never had), she just felt you should at least be given a chance. She felt if we had become so close just through the mail, we certainly had the makings of a compatible relationship, and besides, he loves you, I know he does. Jean is my biggest obstacle.

But I'm sorry, Gar, what's done is done and even though I do love you, I love Don too. Like I said before, he's here and he's now.

It's really going to take me a while to be able to walk on the beach or go out to the bluffs to sit without thinking of you – you've always been with me in both places for the past year.

I'm going to close for now ,G ,and I'm sorry to say this will be my last letter to you. Don has known about you and I writing since the day I met him, but now he is the one man in my life and he feels he would rather not have me writing to another man. I know that seems harsh, but I guess we both should put our past behind us and get on with the future.

Please take care of yourself and remember that I'll never forget our year together. Love you, as always, Patty.

I read and re-read the words over and over again, "*this will be my last letter to you...,*" it was hard to accept and harder to understand. I knew Patty too well—we had lived together for a year and been each others daily diary, how could we just write good-bye?

I loved Patty...a love that we shared. A love not shared by many people. Ours was not a love of intimacy, but a love of friendship, a love of mutual caring, and a love of feelings. Our dreams were real. They would lead us on to possibly other feelings with other meanings, but for now we shared a closeness of family and a caring defined by the word friendship. She meant more to me than any other girl I had dated, or any friend I ever had because of one word...caring.

I guess that's why the shock of these last two letters devastated me so much. I knew her too well, or at least I thought I did. But because of our relationship and because she saved my life in Vietnam, I would abide by her wishes and stop writing. I would hear those words echoing for the last eight months of my service duty, but my respect for Patty and our relationship, convinced me to abide by her wishes. I came home from Nam, a place where so many of my buddies died, hoping never to face death again. But here I was facing another loss, the death of a dream that had kept me alive for so long. Our dream had died...our rendezvous on the beach was never to be.

On September 21, 1968, I was honorably discharged from the USMC and became what is considered by many to be better than a Marine—I became an ex-Marine. Over the next year I wrote two letters to Pensacola, one to Patty's family and one to Doretta, their housekeeper. I did not want to interfere; I simply asked them to let me know how Patty was doing and if her life was a happy one. I never received an answer to either letter.

Good-bye, Patty...I love you. And thanks for caring!

EPILOGUE

This book was a hard book to write. When I was discharged from the Marine Corp the subject of Vietnam and my experiences were pushed to the back of my mind and never brought up in conversation. Once I decided to write the book, I had to pull those memories back out and bring them to the written page. The loss of my comrades always brings tears to my eyes, and I still find it very hard to go to the Vietnam Wall in Washington and see those names.

The first question I am always asked after someone reads the book is, "Did you ever meet or talk to Patty again?" So, I have decided to address that question for everyone who is interested in "the rest of the story."

You can go to my online website at www.GLUSBYbooks.com, and I will have a page there called *TFC – The Sequel*. It will tell you what happened with Patty and I...if anything??

Printed in the United States
21455LVS00002B/181-225

9 781413 733976